THE ODDS GET EVEN

NATALE GHENT

THE ODDS GET EVEN

HarperTrophyCanada™
An imprint of HarperCollinsPublishersLtd

The Odds Get Even
Copyright © 2009 by Natale Ghent.
All rights reserved.

Published by Harper*Trophy*Canada™, an imprint
of HarperCollins Publishers Ltd

First published by HarperCollins Publishers Ltd
in an original trade paperback edition: 2009
This digest paperback edition: 2010

Harper*Trophy*Canada™ is a trademark of HarperCollins Publishers

HarperCollins books may be purchased for educational, business, or sales
promotional use through our Special Markets Department.

HarperCollins Publishers Ltd
2 Bloor Street East, 20th Floor
Toronto, Ontario, Canada
M4W 1A8

www.harpercollins.ca

Library and Archives Canada Cataloguing in Publication

Ghent, Natale, 1962–
The odds get even / Natale Ghent.

ISBN 978-1-55468-415-1

I. Title.
PS8563.H46O34 2010   jC813'.6   C2010-900828-6

Printed and bound in the United States

HC 9 8 7 6 5 4 3 2 1

For Wesley and Brian.
And for odd fellows, young and old, everywhere.

CHAPTER ONE

THE ODD FELLOWS

It was a quiet Sunday afternoon on Green Bottle Street when Boney climbed the rope ladder into the clubhouse to find his friend Squeak sitting at Lookout #1, scanning the horizon with his antique brass telescope. At the other end of the clubhouse, Boney's friend Itchy sprawled like an exhausted octopus in a chair at the table, slurping on a cherry slush.

"Anything to report?" Boney asked.

Squeak lowered his telescope. "It's odd," he whistled through the large gap in his front teeth. "Everything is quiet . . . a little too quiet."

Just as he said this, a rain of eggs pelted the Odd Fellows' clubhouse.

"Fire in the hole!" Squeak shouted as he dived to the floor, eggs hitting the clubhouse in a shower of yellow yolk and slippery, slimy white.

One egg made it cleanly through a window, hitting Itchy square in the forehead. Boney would have been splattered too, but he quickly hit the deck, the egg shrapnel shattering over his head and smearing across the floor behind him.

And then they heard it: that horrible, familiar voice cackling hoarsely below.

"Ha ha ha ha ha ha ha! Take that, you losers!"

Boney jumped up and shot his head out the window. "Fart King!" he screamed. "Why don't you and your merry men take a hike!"

The egg bombers laughed all the louder as they disappeared on their bikes along the length of train tracks that ran behind the houses on Green Bottle Street.

"Take a hike . . . ?" Itchy said, egg yolk dripping down his cheeks. "I bet that really hurt their feelings." He ran his hand across his face, drawing back blood-red fingers. "Ahhh! I'm bleeding!" he shouted, jumping to his feet. "Look at me! I'm covered in blood!"

Squeak ran his finger through the red goop on Itchy's face, then stuck it in his mouth. "Mmmmm . . . cherry," he said, smacking his lips.

"It's only your red slush," Boney pointed out.

Itchy collapsed with relief into his chair. Squeak blinked at him thoughtfully from behind his Coke-bottle-bottom aviator goggles, which nearly swallowed his whole face and were held on with a leather safety strap that ran around the back of his small, round head. The goggles were authentic, from a World War I cache. The lenses were modified with someone's prescription—but not Squeak's. This made it difficult for Squeak to navigate through the world, and gave his eyes the appearance of two blue goldfish swimming aimlessly behind the thick lenses. Why he insisted on wearing the goggles was a mystery to everyone except Squeak. He picked up a rag and began dabbing gently at Itchy's hair.

"It's the third time you've been hit this week," he said.

Boney picked up a rag and began dabbing at Itchy's hair as well. He knew things would be different if only they weren't all so . . . *odd.*

No one was quite certain what it was that made Boney odd, including himself. It wasn't his long chin, or the hare-brained schemes he cooked up. It wasn't the fact that his parents had disappeared in a ballooning accident while chasing down some scientific curiosity when Boney was just a baby, leaving him in the care of his aunt and uncle, who didn't know the first thing about raising a child. It wasn't his nickname, Boney, which often made people laugh. It wasn't anything anyone could put a finger on, but rather some kind of invisible "odd" signal Boney emitted that other people received—even people who were meeting him for the very first time. His friends Itchy and Squeak felt it too, but then again, they were odd as well.

Itchy was far too skinny, with feet the size of toboggans and a mop of hair so tangled and orange it looked as though it would ignite at any second. Squeak resembled a begoggled and gap-toothed gerbil and was far too smart for his own good, which meant he was almost always misunderstood. Even his teachers never really knew what he was talking about, leaving him no option but to escape in his books and special-effects magazines. So the three boys made a pact to stick together through thick and thin, as they said—a company of Odd Fellows.

Besides being the very best of friends, the Odds were further tethered by the fact that all three were only children, and all three had always lived side by side in a row of crooked little houses on a small street called Green Bottle: house numbers 23, 25, and 27. There were only twelve houses total on Green Bottle, six on either side. And everyone on Green Bottle was old, except for Boney, Itchy, and Squeak, who were the only children on the block. Even more surprising, though, was the fact that all three of their birthdays were less than a week apart in the month of May.

The Odd Fellows agreed that being odd wouldn't be so bad if only people would leave them alone. But they wouldn't. Teachers singled them out in class. Fellow students tormented them ruthlessly. Even the paperboy seemed to have it in for them. But no one was worse than their mortal enemy, Larry Harry, aka *the Fart King*. The Odds called him this because Larry had the peculiar talent of being able to break wind on command — and did so at every opportunity. What's more, he never travelled alone. He enjoyed the constant company of Jones and Jones, identical twin bullies with the collective IQ of a wilted carrot.

And so it was necessary to take precautions. Like always being on the ready for attacks from marauders, and building a clubhouse high up in the oak tree in Boney's backyard, with no fewer than three escape hatches and five special lookout posts that together afforded a full-length view of Green Bottle Street.

Improvements were always being made, like the addition of a roll-up ladder for Escape Hatch #1, and the installation of a fire pole (a length of old plumbing pipe) in Escape Hatch #2. Escape Hatch #3 was currently just a hole in the clubhouse floor with no way to descend except by accident, but plans were in the works for something very innovative — even if the Odds didn't quite know what that was yet. They'd already added a shelf for their reference library, and a new roof made from discarded boards, shingled with margarine tub lids from Boney's aunt's kitchen. The roof helped protect the Odds from the rain—and the eggs thrown by Larry Harry. There was a mop and rags and a bucket of fresh water in the clubhouse at all times for cleanup, and a cooler for milk and soda. But no matter what improvements they made to their clubhouse, somehow the Odds always came out holding the short end of the stick.

"I'm hungry," Itchy announced.

Itchy was always hungry. And itchy. That's how he'd got his name. Even his parents called him that because he scratched at his pale, freckled skin all the time like a dog chasing a flea. He could never sit still, either, so that even when he wasn't scratching you had the feeling he was.

"Check the larder," Boney ordered.

"I already did," Itchy said. "It's empty. We ate the peanut butter and crackers last night."

"Every last crumb?" Boney asked.

Itchy nodded.

Squeak dipped his tasting finger in a puddle of yellow yolk on the floor and brought it up to his nose. "Smells very loud," he said. "Almost deafening."

"Huh?" Itchy said.

"The egg yolk . . . it smells very loud."

Itchy turned to Boney. "What's he talking about?"

Boney shrugged as he continued to dab at his friend's hair.

"I thought it would be cool to have synesthesia," Squeak explained.

Itchy scratched at his elbow. "Sin-a-what?"

"Synesthesia. It's a condition characterized by using different sensory descriptions that are often incompatible."

Itchy looked to Boney for help. "I still don't know what he's talking about."

"It's quite simple," Squeak said. "Synesthetes, as they are called, are able to *smell* colours, *see* sounds, and employ many other possible combinations of senses in addition to their regular senses. I believe the great inventor Leonardo da Vinci was one, though I have no direct proof. But I've read every book about him and by him, including *The Complete Works of Leonardo da Vinci*, a ten-volume set I intend to own some day—"

"Squeak!" Itchy shouted. "What has that got to do with our situation?"

Squeak blinked indignantly from behind his goggles. "I just thought it would be cool to have something like that."

"What would be cool is if we didn't get creamed with eggs by that wretched Fart King and his Demented

Duo, Jones and Jones. They've been bombing us with eggs ever since we entered our scrambled-egg-making machine in the Invention Convention in grade three."

"The Scramb-o-nater," Squeak remembered wistfully. "We would have won if Larry hadn't sabotaged our entry by putting rotten eggs in the refrigerated holding bin. I felt bad for the judges."

"I've never seen adults barf like that before," Boney said, shaking his head.

Itchy jumped up and began pacing the clubhouse floor. "That creep sabotages our invention every year—it's the only reason he ever wins." He smacked his pale fist in the palm of his hand. "I'm so sick of it. I want revenge!"

Boney rolled his eyes. "You say that every year, but then you chicken out whenever I come up with a plan."

"I really mean it this time," Itchy said. "I want to get even."

"How?" Squeak asked.

"I don't know." Itchy deflated into his chair and began scratching absently at his arm again.

"We could win the Invention Convention once and for all," Squeak said. "We're in senior public school now. If we win this year, we'll get to go to the international convention in San Diego. It's the best possible revenge."

"I'm not so sure about that," Itchy muttered.

"We could dare them," Boney suggested.

"What do you mean?" Itchy asked, squinting his eyes with suspicion.

"We could dare them to meet us at the Old Mill. They'll never go there."

"Maybe that's because it's haunted," Itchy said.

"That has never been proved," Squeak countered.

Itchy sat up violently in his chair. "Oh, no?" He held his hand out, counting off examples on his fingers. "What about those three kids who went missing? Or all the campfires people have reported seeing at the mill that seem to spring up on their own? Or how about the weird noises heard coming out of the ruins? Or the rocks thrown at people out of nowhere? Or the creepy groups of robed beings holding seances inside the ruins every Hallowe'en? Are all those reports just made up?"

"We could bring protection," Boney offered.

"Like what? Garlic?" Itchy demanded.

"That only works for vampires — not ghosts," Squeak said.

Boney frowned. "I don't know. But I'll think of something."

"Forget it," Itchy said. "We've never gone to the Old Mill before. Why should we start now?"

"What about you, Squeak?" Boney asked his friend.

"You're not afraid to go to the mill, right?"

Squeak blinked silently back.

"He's terrified," Itchy answered for him. "We all are. Except you."

"How will we know for sure if it's haunted if we don't go and see for ourselves?" Boney said. "We need scientific proof. We have to test the ghost theory if we want to know for sure. Besides, it can't be that scary, can it?"

"That's what those kids who went missing thought," Itchy retorted heatedly. "Then they got vaporized by the ghost. You can count me out."

"That also has never been proved," Squeak said. He retrieved a small spiral notebook from the green canvas military messenger bag he kept strapped over his shoulder at all times. Opening the notebook, he began reading aloud from his entry on the Old Mill. "Established in 1827, the mill was situated at the confluence of two rivers: the Speed and the Eramosa . . ."

"Squeak!" Itchy shouted in frustration. "What has that got to do with ghosts or missing boys?"

Squeak shot him a piercing look. "I was getting to that. I thought you would appreciate some background information, but apparently I'm mistaken."

"Maybe you'd better skip to the good stuff," Boney said. "I mean . . . the stuff concerning the matter at hand."

Squeak nodded, skimming feverishly through ten or twelve pages of notes written in very tiny script, complete with pen-and-ink drawings, footnotes, and margin annotations.

"Give me that!" Itchy said, grabbing the notebook.

The two boys wrestled for a few moments, until the notebook fell to the floor at Boney's feet.

"I'll read it," Boney said. He picked up the flashlight he kept hanging on the clubhouse wall and clicked it on, aiming the beam eerily beneath his chin. The light in the clubhouse seemed to suddenly darken. Boney spoke in a haunted voice for full effect.

"The mill, long since abandoned, has been the subject of much controversial paranormal activity. Legend has it that three runaway teenage boys disappeared in 1952 after spending the night camped out in the old ruins of the once magnificent building. No trace of the boys was ever found, except for a pair of glasses and a sneaker. Though never proved professionally, it is rumoured that moaning and whispering can be heard on the full moon of every month, and several eyewitnesses have reported the smell of burning wood, and the crackling glow of a campfire . . ." Boney's voice shrank to a whisper as he spoke these last words. He looked up from the page, fixing his gaze on his friends. There was an unnerving silence, soon broken by an indignant Itchy.

"This is insane! Why would we ever go there?"

Itchy looked to Squeak for support, but Squeak simply gazed out the clubhouse window.

Boney stared at the notebook, pulling absently on his long chin. "The full moon . . ." he murmured.

"Forget it!" Itchy said. "It's crazy. I won't have anything to do with it."

"You don't even know what I'm thinking about!" Boney said.

"I don't have to know," Itchy quipped, mimicking Boney's mannerisms. "Whenever you start pulling on your chin and thinking, it means trouble. So whatever you have in mind, I'm not interested."

"You were the one who said you wanted revenge."

"Yeah, but I don't want to get myself killed."

"Why do you think I'd get you killed?"

Itchy scoffed. "Oh, I don't know. Maybe because you almost drowned us once when you wanted to test the 'durability' of a boat you found at the dump. Or how about the time you thought it was a great idea for us to jump off the roof of your house using pillowcases as parachutes?"

"That was back in grade four," Boney said, defensively.

"Or how about the time you wanted to see if magnifying glasses really can start fires and practically burned the school down?" Itchy demanded. "That was last week!"

Boney waved dismissively. "It worked, didn't it? Besides, everything we've done has been performed in the name of science."

"Science!" Itchy shouted. "How old are we?"

"Eleven," Boney said.

"Yeah, eleven! And we want to live to be at least twelve. You've almost killed us a hundred times since we were born—all in the name of science!"

There was a pause in the argument as Boney considered Itchy's accusation.

After a very long while, Squeak, who had been blinking and staring at his two friends, got up and moved toward Escape Hatch #2.

"Where are you going?" Itchy barked.

"Home," Squeak said. "I want to begin work on our invention for the convention."

Boney's eyes widened. "You have an idea already?"

"Of course," Squeak said. "But nothing I care to divulge at this time." With that, he grabbed his notebook from Boney's hand, blinked, and disappeared down the pole.

A second later, there was a small shout from the bottom of the tree. Boney and Itchy peered through the escape hatch to find Squeak lying in a heap on the ground at the base of the pole, his goggles askew on his face.

"I'm all right," he called up, then stood, adjusted the goggles, brushed himself off, and promptly walked into the base of the tree.

"I'm all right," he said again.

Itchy and Boney watched as Squeak drifted from the backyard toward the shed.

"Veer right!" Boney called down.

Squeak adjusted his trajectory just before stumbling off the walk into the garden.

"I wonder what his invention idea is," Itchy mused, slurping loudly on the straw of his empty slush.

"I don't know, but I bet it'll be good—as long as Larry Harry doesn't sabotage it."

"It's not just Larry Harry we have to worry about," Itchy said. "The convention entries get better every year. That weenie Edward Wormer has some good ideas. And Simon Biddle, too. Stacy Karns is also pretty smart. And it doesn't hurt that she collaborates with fifteen of her friends."

"Don't worry about Wormer and Biddle," Boney said. "They're just amateurs. Squeak can out-think those guys any day. And Stacy can collaborate with as many friends as she likes, she'll never come close to Squeak's brilliance. His ideas are truly inspired. It's like the ghost of Leonardo da Vinci whispers in his ear or something. I wish that would happen to me."

"William!" Boney's aunt shouted from the kitchen window. "Dinnertime!"

Boney groaned.

"I'm off too, then," Itchy said, stepping gingerly around the egg on the floor of the clubhouse. "There's no food here anyway."

"Right," Boney said, still absorbed in thoughts of revenge against the egg bombers.

Itchy wrapped his skinny legs around the escape pole and slid out of sight. Boney remained, thinking deeply, until his aunt hollered out the kitchen window again. Then he slid down the pole as well.

CHAPTER TWO

CANNED SOUP

In the kitchen, Boney's aunt ladled a big, sticky heap of something orange and oozing onto his plate. "You've been spending far too much time in that clubhouse of yours, young man," she said. "Have you even looked at your homework?"

Boney stared at the steaming pile in front of him. "We were discussing our invention for the convention."

"Always with the science," his aunt clucked. "You're going to end up just like your father."

"Mildred!" Boney's uncle admonished from behind his paper. He was reading the stock exchange pages, as usual. He had a job at a bank as a small-loans officer, and he was always going on about the price of this and that, despite the fact that no one else seemed to care, least of all his wife, whose sole purpose in life, Boney believed, was to kill every insect in existence and to create the worst-tasting food on the planet with canned soup. She'd even threatened to write a cookbook.

Boney poked cautiously at the orange goop with his fork. "What is this?"

"It's *Busy Day Casserole*." His aunt beamed.

"Another soup-can recipe?" Boney asked with dismay.

"It's a wonderful meal, full of nutrition and time-saving goodness."

"So . . . it's spaghetti with soup," Boney said.

"Pasta," his aunt corrected him.

"Don't sass back, boy," his uncle muttered. "There are hungry children in the world who would love to have such a fine meal." He flapped his newspaper dramatically, folding it into a neat square before depositing it on the chair beside him. His face instantly drooped as his eyes fell upon the steaming pile of orange goop on his own plate. He and Boney exchanged looks of dread. His uncle took a tentative taste of the goop, his mouth contorting in disgust. He pointed to the garbage behind Boney.

Boney grabbed two teaspoons from the table and pressed them over his eyes in an attempt to distract his aunt so his uncle could ditch the food. "Look! I'm an alien!"

But his aunt was not so easily fooled. "What nonsense!" she said, snatching the spoons from Boney's eyes and handing him a napkin.

Boney began to eat, pinching his nose. His uncle did the same, but he refrained from holding his own nose. They shovelled the casserole into their mouths as though they were starving.

"Now, no need to wolf your food," his aunt said, standing by the table with the red gingham tea towel she kept permanently fixed over her arm. "There's plenty more in the oven." Her gaze suddenly shot up to the ceiling. "Do you hear that buzzing?" she asked.

"Uh-uhnn," Boney and his uncle mumbled in unison, shoving the food into their cheeks until they looked like chipmunks.

"Robert?" Boney's aunt said, her voice tinged with hysteria. "Do you hear that buzzing? There's a bug in here somewhere." She began jumping around the room, snapping her tea towel wildly at the ceiling. "There it is!" she shrieked as a housefly zipped across the kitchen. "Get it, Robert!"

Boney's uncle craned his neck toward the ceiling as his wife leapt and shouted, cracking the tea towel with shocking force, snapping a row of empty glass jars from the top of the kitchen cupboards to the floor with a horrible crash.

"Now, now, Mildred," Boney's uncle spluttered through his moustache.

"May I be excused?" Boney mumbled, his mouth stuffed to capacity with canned-soup casserole. He didn't wait for an answer but bolted from the table, leaving his aunt and uncle to contend with the fly and the broken jars.

Upstairs in the bathroom, Boney spat the casserole into the toilet and flushed. His real mother would have never made him eat such horrible things, he thought, as he rinsed his mouth with water. Then he ran to his room and unearthed a jawbreaker from his sock drawer to help remove the awful metallic soup-can taste.

Moments later, he heard the toilet flush again, and his uncle's horrified face appeared in the doorway of his room. "Got another one of those jawbreakers?" he asked. He shuddered as Boney searched through his sock drawer and produced another candy. "It'll be our secret," his uncle whispered, pressing his finger over his lips as he closed the door to Boney's room.

When his uncle was gone, Boney went over to his window and lifted the end of the Tele-tube to his lips. The Tele-tube was one of Squeak's inventions: a clear, flexible, plastic tube that connected the boys' rooms and functioned as a means of covert communication without adult detection. Their houses were narrow, and all the boys had bedrooms facing the backyard. That meant that each of them was able to run a length of tubing through holes drilled in the sash of their windows (courtesy of Squeak and his father's tools), and run the tubes between the branches of the elm trees that grew in identical fashion between each pair of houses, concealing them from prying eyes. What's more, Boney and Itchy kept towels at the ready to hide the ends of the Tele-tube should the grown-ups come into their rooms. Squeak didn't need to worry about parental detection because his father was an electrician and worked so much he was never home for long, and his mother was gone, having left to join a travelling cabaret when Squeak was just a child—a fact Boney's aunt would never let anyone forget.

The Tele-tube was light-years beyond the boys' earlier Dixie cup system, which Squeak deemed "antiquated," and which required louder voices and constant vigilance to prevent the string from tangling, especially when Itchy's fox terrier, Snuff, was on the prowl. The only drawback to the Tele-tube was that Squeak, who lived in the middle at 25 Green Bottle, had to relay messages from Boney at 23 to Itchy at 27. But since Squeak was free from parental scrutiny, he simply ran lengths of tubing from both his bedroom windows so that he could talk to Boney and Itchy simultaneously from the comfort of his bed.

Boney leaned toward the end of the Tele-tube, opening his mouth to speak. But instead of words, a giant burp erupted and rumbled along the length of the tube into Squeak's room.

"Uhhhh!" Squeak howled from the other end of the tube. "Sounds putrid! Smells like anguish."

"Sorry," Boney apologized.

"Another soup-can recipe?" Squeak asked.

Boney stifled another burp. "It was orange this time. What kind of soup is orange?"

"Perhaps it was cheddar cheese soup," Squeak answered thoughtfully.

"What did you have for dinner?" Boney asked.

"Same as every night." Squeak sighed. "TV dinner. It's the only thing my dad knows how to make. And he doesn't do it very well. The peas were still frozen in the tray and the Salisbury steak was like a hockey puck. Dad was going to take them back to the grocery store until he realized he hadn't turned on the oven. Then he realized the oven was broken, so he just soaked the trays under hot water in the sink."

"Eeeehhh . . ."

"I just wish he'd let me cook. I'm actually quite good at it. But he insists on cooking when he's home. I guess it makes him feel more like a parent."

"Sounds like you could use a jawbreaker." Boney found another in his sock drawer and pushed it into the mouth of the tube, lifting the end so the jawbreaker rolled along the length between the two windows.

"Thanks," Squeak said. There was a rustling sound

from Squeak's end of the tube. "Itchy wants to know what's going on," he relayed to Boney.

"Tell him I have a plan for revenge."

There was a pause, then Squeak's voice floated through the tube again. "He doesn't like the sound of it."

"I haven't even told him what it is yet," Boney scoffed. "Tell him he has to do it. It's the element of surprise we need here."

Another pause.

"He says he's not going to the haunted mill," Squeak reported.

"It doesn't involve the mill or ghosts or anything!" Boney yelled, growing irritated with Itchy's stubbornness.

Squeak was just about to relay Boney's message when Boney's aunt was heard calling up from the bottom of the stairs.

"William? What's going on up there?" And then the distinct sound of high heels climbing the steps.

"Red alert!" Boney shouted into the tube. "Adult approaching. I'll pick you up tomorrow for school." Boney tossed the towel over the Tele-tube, jumped into bed fully dressed, and snapped out his light just as his aunt burst through the door to check on him.

She gazed suspiciously around the room, but found Boney sleeping peacefully.

Once his aunt was gone, Boney changed into his pyjamas and uncovered the Tele-tube, whispering, "Good night, Squeak. Good night, Itchy." He covered the tube and climbed into bed as Squeak's small voice floated into the room.

"Goodnight, Boney."

Boney nestled in to sleep, but not before releasing another horrible, smelly, orange burp.

"Ugh," he winced. "Canned soup."

CHAPTER THREE

A Ghostly Idea

The next morning, Boney rushed out the door to collect Squeak and Itchy for school. He waved to Mr. Johnson across the street, who was already up and mowing his perfectly manicured lawn. He jumped to avoid Mrs. Pulmoni's cat, who streaked across the street with Itchy's dog, Snuff, in wild pursuit. He ducked to avoid the rolled newspaper thrown carelessly by the paperboy, but he got hit in the back of the head all the same by a second paper as he approached Squeak's place.

"You should duck," Squeak said, appearing around the corner of his house, dragging a large can of garbage to the curb.

"I swear he aims right at me," Boney grumbled, grabbing a handle on the can to help. "I forgot it's garbage day."

"You forget every week," Squeak said. He held his wrist up to his goggled eyes and peered at his watch.

"If you hurry, you have time to take it out so you don't get in trouble when you get home after school today."

Boney raced back and dragged the can of garbage from behind his garage to the curb, stepping quickly aside to avoid Mr. Peterson, who zipped past on his bike, bell ringing, the way he did every morning on his way to work.

"Have you noticed he always rings his bell after he nearly runs us down?" Boney complained. "We'd better hurry up and get Itchy or we'll be late for school."

Itchy wasn't waiting on his porch when his friends arrived. As usual, he was nowhere to be seen. But his dog, Snuff, was there. Snuff ran up to the boys, growling viciously at Boney.

"I hate that dog," Boney said.

Squeak leaned over and picked the dog up. "But he's so sweet," he laughed as Snuff happily licked his face.

"Well, he hates me." Boney reached to pet Snuff, but the dog growled angrily. "See? He really *hates* me."

"Maybe that's because you fell on him when he was a puppy."

"It wasn't my fault! I tripped."

"You were chasing him."

"He took my favourite baseball cap."

"He was only a puppy," Squeak said. "He didn't know any better. I hope someday you two can be friends."

"Don't hold your breath." Boney tramped up the stairs to Itchy's house. "What would happen if Itchy was actually on time for once?" he asked as he rang the bell.

Squeak pondered his friend's question. "I believe there'd be a rift in the space-time continuum and life as we know it would end."

The front door swung open and Itchy's father appeared, wearing gold glasses and a tight-fitting white spandex Elvis outfit, with sequins sparkling around the cuffs. The boys weren't the least bit surprised to see Itchy's dad dressed like this. He'd been impersonating Elvis since long before the three boys were even born. They weren't sure exactly how much work there was in such a field, but Mr. Schutz always seemed to have somewhere to go.

"My fans are here," he said in his best Elvis voice. He pointed dramatically at Boney and started singing "You Ain't Nothin' but a Hound Dog."

This made Snuff yelp, and he leapt from Squeak's arms, streaking into the house.

"Hi, Mr. Schutz," the boys chimed.

"Big day today," Mr. Schutz said, striking a pose and giving a wide, toothy smile. "I'm making my debut at

the Bingo Hall tonight. Gonna give the ladies a thrill."
He gyrated his hips, running a hand through his greasy
black hair.

"Uhhh . . . that's great, Mr. Schutz," Boney said. "Is
Itchy ready?"

"Itchy, Itchy, Itchy . . ." Mr. Schutz snapped his fingers repeatedly as though trying to recall the name. "Oh,
yes. The boy. Itchy!" he yelled up the stairs.

When Itchy appeared, his father swung the door
wide and ushered him out, handing him a bag of garbage on the way.

"Itchy has left the building," he said, then added,
"Thank you. Thank you very much," before slamming
the door.

The door instantly opened again and Itchy's mother
appeared in a bright-purple bathrobe. She handed Itchy
a quarter for candy apple day — Itchy's favourite day of
the school year — then kissed him on the head. "Have a
good day at school, dear," she said. "Oh, and Boney . . .
could you thank your aunt for the soup-can recipe? I've
added it to the dozen others she's given me." She smiled
and closed the door again.

Boney turned to Itchy in horror. "Does she actually
use those recipes?"

"Never. She's too busy redecorating all the time."
Itchy tugged at his bright-purple T-shirt.

"Nice," Boney said.

Itchy rolled his eyes. "It's my mom's latest favourite colour. She dyed everything in the house purple."

"It sets off your hair," Squeak mused.

Itchy ignored him, pushing his candy apple quarter into his pocket. "Did you guys bring money for candy apples?" he asked, hopefully.

Squeak and Boney shook their heads.

"You're the only one of us who likes them," Squeak reminded him.

"Ehhh . . . yeah," Boney agreed. "They're really kind of disgusting."

Itchy's jaw dropped. "Disgusting? I love them. All that gooey red candy goodness."

Boney cringed. "You'd think you'd hate them after last time, when Larry threw one at you and it stuck in your hair."

"It was fine after I washed it."

"It took you an hour to pick the hair off the apple," Squeak said.

"Yuck." Boney shuddered as the boys stomped down the stairs to make their way to school.

The Odds walked along the sidewalk, Squeak drifting dangerously close to the curb as the garbage truck roared around the corner. It jerked loudly to a stop and a man in blue coveralls jumped out, tipped a few cans into the back of the truck, then threw the empty cans to the sidewalk, narrowly missing the three boys, who jumped in unison to avoid getting hit. The truck lurched forward to the next house.

"I've ordered blood capsules that look so real, even rescue workers can't tell the difference," Squeak suddenly announced. "And I got these, through mail order." He held up a small black-and-red box. "Alcatraz Prison Cards. Each one has mug shots and statistics for some of the most famous prisoners ever to stay at Alcatraz. I thought they'd make a nice addition to our reference library."

"Cool," Boney said.

"Weird," Itchy added.

Squeak opened the box excitedly. "But you know what the weirdest thing of all is? The first prisoner in the box is a guy called Harry Larry!"

Itchy stopped in his tracks. "What do you mean?"

"It's true," Squeak said, holding up a card. "He was caught stealing mail."

Boney and Itchy grabbed the card from Squeak's hand and studied the black-and-white picture.

"'Prisoner 95,'" Boney read aloud. "'Violation of postal laws, stealing mail. Sentence: six years.' It'd be just like Larry to do something like that."

"It even kind of looks like him," Itchy said.

"Do you think he's a relative of Larry's?" Boney asked. "I mean . . . the name's backwards, but you never know with this kind of stuff. Criminals are always changing their names around."

"Maybe he reincarnated and came back as Larry Harry," Squeak joked.

"Either that, or Larry's mother has a sick sense of humour," Itchy said.

Boney laughed. "Prisoner 95 . . . the name suits him."

"Yeah, because he's probably going to end up in jail eventually." Itchy handed the card back to Squeak. "Who else is in there? Jones and Jones?"

Squeak shuffled through the cards. "All the big names: Al Capone, Machine Gun Kelly, the Bird Man of Alcatraz. But I haven't had a chance to read all the cards yet."

"Why not?" Boney asked as the three boys turned the corner toward school.

"Because I spent the night thinking about our invention for the convention. It's only a month and a half away, you know."

"Maybe you could tell us what you're working on?" Itchy asked.

Squeak blinked thoughtfully from behind his goggles. "An apparitions sensor—an Apparator, for short."

Boney and Itchy stared blankly back at him.

"A ghost detector," Squeak clarified for his friends.

"Oh, no . . ." Itchy said. "Not with the ghosts again. I can't stand it!"

"How does it work?" Boney asked.

"Don't tell him," Itchy moaned, pulling at his flaming orange hair.

"It senses electromagnetic disturbances," Squeak explained. "It seems ghosts leave a trail behind — like a snail — only electromagnetically, when they move through space. I read about it in *Ghost Hunters* magazine." He pulled the magazine from his bag.

"What do you need to build it?" Boney asked.

"Not much at all: a capacitor from an old tube radio, some copper wire, a toggle switch, some kind of handle — preferably Bakelite — a standard Weller forty-watt iron, some Deans ultra-connectors, a couple rare earth magnets, and a dual-polarity air ion detector. No one has ever done anything like this before at our school."

Itchy's pale face grew even paler. "Don't I have a say in this? What if I don't *want* to build a ghost detector?"

"First prize is five hundred dollars," Squeak said. "I overheard Mr. Harvey telling Principal Loadman they're increasing the prize money to encourage more students to enter the competition."

Itchy's face lit up.

"Then we'll need hard facts for our convention entry," Boney said. "We can do field research at the haunted mill once we build the Apparator."

Itchy's face fell. "Oh, great." He kicked angrily at a stone on the sidewalk. It shot through the air, ricocheting loudly off the door of a shiny red convertible double-parked in front of the school.

Boney's eyes widened. "Itchy . . . that's Prisoner 95's car you just dinged."

"That's the prisoner's *father's* car he just dinged," Squeak corrected him, seconds before his *Ghost Hunters* magazine was snatched from his hands.

"What do you think you're doing?" an angry voice demanded.

The Odds spun around and found themselves face to face with their mortal enemy, Larry Harry.

CHAPTER FOUR

PRISONER 95

Larry stood in front of the school, bookended by his henchmen, Jones and Jones. The twins were wearing identical brown sweaters and had matching soup-bowl haircuts; their faces were splattered with freckles. The schoolyard swarmed loudly with students.

"I asked you a question, *doofus*," Larry sneered at Itchy. "If I find one little scratch on my dad's car, you're going to get it. And what's with the stupid purple shirt, son of Elvis?"

Jones and Jones howled with laughter.

"Give back our magazine," Boney said.

"Make me," Larry taunted. He looked briefly at the zombies on the cover. "What is this, Bonehead? Your family album?"

"Just give it back," Boney insisted. "Or else."

"Did you hear that?" Larry said, looking at Jones and Jones. "Bonehead is threatening *me*."

He took a step closer to Boney, who bravely stood his ground. Itchy and Squeak took several steps back.

"I don't like the smell of this," Squeak said. "It smells like danger."

"Smells like what?" Larry growled, looming in Squeak's face.

Squeak stared at the tops of his running shoes. "Like d-danger," he stuttered.

Larry gave Squeak a shove. "What are you, some kind of nutter?"

"He's not a nutter," Boney defended his friend. "It's syne . . . something, a condition that makes you muddle things up a bit . . . anyway, it's not real."

"Sounds stupid to me," Larry scoffed, turning to his sidekicks for approval.

"Yeah, sounds stupid!" Jones and Jones guffawed.

Squeak pushed nervously at the bridge of his goggles. "Actually, it's a condition characterized by access to different sensory perceptions that are often apparently incompatible—"

"How would you like me to make your head incompatible with your neck?" Larry snarled.

Just then the bell rang, sending kids shrieking and running into the school. Miss Sours, the boys' homeroom teacher, appeared, lurching toward the group like a reanimated corpse.

"What's going on here?" she sniffed, her rhinestone cat's-eye glasses perched on the end of her pointed nose.

Larry handed the magazine back to Boney. "Thanks," he said pleasantly, as though Boney were his best friend.

Miss Sours scowled. "You heard the bell," she snapped. "Get to class."

"Sure thing, Miss Sours," Larry said. He turned to Itchy. "No hard feelings, eh, Red?" He clapped Itchy forcefully on the back, crushing an egg over his purple shirt.

Jones and Jones roared as they ran with Larry toward the school.

"My shirt!" Itchy moaned. "That filthy criminal crushed an egg on my shirt!"

"Stupid jerk," Boney cursed.

"At least he didn't hit you in the face with it," Squeak said.

"Gee, that's a relief," Itchy scoffed. "How am I supposed to go to school covered in egg?"

"Why don't you change into your gym shirt?" Squeak suggested.

"Because my gym shirt is covered in dirt from when Jones and Jones dragged me through the mud," Itchy groaned.

"That was last week," Boney said.

"So, my mom hasn't done laundry yet, has she?" Itchy snapped.

"Perhaps you should learn how to run the washing machine yourself," Squeak advised.

"Perhaps I should learn how to fight." Itchy kicked at the air with his skinny white legs.

"Ah . . . maybe not," Boney said.

"You can wear my gym shirt," Squeak offered. "I never wear it, so it's clean. I've still got that get-out-of-gym-permanently note my dad wrote me."

"Yeah, how'd you pull that off, anyway?" Boney asked.

"I told him it interfered with my studies. And my vision's not so good." He pointed to his goggles and smiled. "Come on, you can change before class starts."

The boys ran to Squeak's locker. Squeak produced his gym shirt and handed it to Itchy.

"Hurry up, or we're going to get a detention," Boney said.

Itchy looked over his shoulder at the other students streaming through the hall. "I'm not changing in front of everybody."

"You have no choice. We don't have time to go to the bathroom."

Itchy shook his head, looked over his shoulder again, then quickly pulled his shirt up over his skinny shoulder blades. A group of girls squealed in horror as they passed.

"Ewwwww!"

Itchy threw his purple shirt to the ground and desperately tried to pull Squeak's shirt on as quickly as possible, but got his head caught in the neck. "It's too small!" he screamed.

Boney grabbed the hem of the T-shirt and yanked with all his might until Itchy's orange mop popped through the neck. The shirt barely covered his stomach and the sleeves bunched horribly under the arms.

"I can't wear this!" Itchy wailed.

"You have no choice," Boney said. "We're going to be late."

The Odds skidded into class, causing Miss Sours to sneer over her glasses. The boys took their seats near the back of the classroom. Itchy hunched at his desk, moping. He tugged on the hem of the shirt to cover his stomach, causing the back to ride halfway to his shoulders. To make matters worse, Larry Harry and Jones and Jones snickered knowingly from their seats on the other side of the room.

"I guess there's a considerable difference in our sizes," Squeak observed.

"This shirt wouldn't fit a doll!" Itchy hissed.

"Silence!" Miss Sours shrieked, slamming a yard-stick on the top of her desk.

Itchy waited until the chalk dust settled before attempting to speak again. He leaned closer to Boney, whispering, "I don't care what it takes, I want revenge."

"You'll get it," Boney promised. "I've got it all planned . . ."

"Are you hard of hearing, Mr. Boneham?" Miss Sours rasped.

Boney, Itchy, and Squeak shot straight up in their seats, along with the rest of the class, assuming their most attentive poses.

"No, ma'am," Boney mumbled.

"Then why are you still talking?" Miss Sours asked. She came out from behind her desk, moving like a wooden cart with square wheels. Jerking her way down the aisle, she held the yardstick in front of her as she walked, swirling it in threatening circles. "I don't want to hear another sound from your end of the room, do you hear me? Not a peep, gurgle, or cheep. Do I make myself clear, Mr. Boneham?" She attempted to smile, her teeth yellow and pointy like a hamster's.

Boney averted his eyes, but when he did, his gaze fell upon a horrific sight: Miss Sours's leg hair, pok-ing like needles through her nylons. It gave her shape-less legs the appearance of two skinny cacti, stumping malevolently along between the desks. The idea was so ridiculous that before he could stop himself, Boney let out a loud and very obnoxious snort. In a flash, the yardstick came down with a sickening crack across his desk.

"Aaaaaghhhh!" he cried in terror.

Jones and Jones burst into gleeful laughter.

Crack! Crack! Miss Sours's yardstick found its mark with alarming precision, silencing Jones and Jones instantly. No one could explain how she could suddenly move so quickly — except Squeak, who believed she was a vampire.

"You find this amusing, hmmmm?" Miss Sours taunted the rest of the class. "I assure you it isn't. The next person who splits so much as a smirk will receive a detention." She squinted across the room, sweeping the length of the class with the yardstick like a sword, daring any of the students to challenge her. Everyone sat petrified, including Jones and Jones.

But when Miss Sours turned her back, Larry looked at Boney and made a slashing motion across his throat.

"Jerk," Itchy muttered.

Crack! Down came the yardstick, and now it was Itchy's turn to be terrorized.

In the minutes before homeroom ended, Miss Sours's yardstick silenced several more students. When the bell rang at last, the entire class bolted from their seats, rushing for the door.

In the hallway, Larry made a point of smashing into Boney as he walked by, and Jones and Jones sent Itchy and Squeak slamming into the lockers.

"I hate those stupid goons," Itchy said, rubbing his shoulder.

"Just be happy they aren't in our math class," Boney said.

"Yes," Squeak piped up, rubbing his own shoulder. "If they weren't so stupid, they wouldn't have all flunked math. And then where would we be?"

Itchy scowled. "I don't see how it could be any worse."

"Believe me, it can be," Boney said. "We start lacrosse in gym today."

CHAPTER FIVE

FOUL PLAY

Waiting for gym class to begin, Itchy and Boney huddled together on the playing field, arms folded, attempting to look inconspicuous. It was the last class of the day.

Itchy tugged on the hem of Squeak's shirt, trying desperately to cover himself. His legs stuck out like pool cues from his giant shorts. His mother bought his shorts two sizes too big, convinced Itchy would grow into them. But he only ever got taller and skinnier, making the shorts look twice as ridiculous. His mismatched socks drooped loosely around his ankles, accentuating his worn sneakers, which looked like long black canvas canoes.

Boney was little better off, but at least his socks matched. He avoided Larry's gaze, pretending to be fascinated by something on the ground. But it was no use. Larry and his goons wouldn't be put off that easily.

"Hey, Bonehead," Larry called out. "I have a message from your mother." He bent over and let out the most disgusting fart. His friends roared with laughter.

"Charming," Boney muttered.

"It's the most intelligent thing he's said all day," Itchy sneered. He tugged at his T-shirt. "It's a good thing gym isn't co-ed. It'd be way worse to get creamed by Larry in front of girls. We'd never live it down."

A sharp whistle blast pierced the air, calling the class to order.

"Listen up!" Mr. Richards, their gym teacher, yelled.

Better known as Colonel R., Mr. Richards had only one volume setting for his voice: loud. And he was never seen without a whistle clenched between his teeth. Even when he talked he never dropped it. He stood before the class, holding a lacrosse stick under one arm.

"It's the start of a brand-new unit," he bellowed. "You all know the rules of lacrosse. We played it last year. And I don't want anyone making like a human target this time, you got that, Red?" He glared at Itchy, whose face instantly burned scarlet.

"Guess you'd better stay outta my way," Larry growled in Itchy's ear.

"Just you watch your back," Boney hissed in Itchy's defence.

"Oooooh, I'm so *scared*," Larry said. "We're gonna make mincemeat outta both of you wimps."

Boney opened his mouth to retaliate, but before he could get a word out, Colonel R.'s whistle split the air again.

"All right! We need captains. Harry, you're captain number one. Jones, you're number two."

"That isn't fair," Itchy whined.

"Did you say something, Red?" Colonel R. demanded.

Itchy shook his head.

Boney leaned toward Itchy. "He doesn't know anybody else's names. Ever wonder why he always calls you Red?"

"Fine," Colonel R. said, pointing to Itchy. "You're number two, Red."

The class let out a collective groan.

"Number two!" Jones and Jones mocked.

"Cut the crap!" Colonel R. roared, which made Jones and Jones laugh even louder. "Now move it and pick your teams!" He gave a piercing blast on his whistle.

"Jones and Jones," Larry called.

"You can't pick two people straight off," Itchy said.

"Who says?" Larry threatened him with a fist.

"Fine," Itchy backed down. "I pick Boney."

"Your loss," he said with a sneer. "I pick Thomas,

Reilly, Wilson, Skrobecki, Grosset, Vertolli, Hadders, and Shean," Larry rhymed off.

The chosen students moved over to Larry's side of the field. Boney surveyed the rest of the class. Only the nerds were left, including Edward Wormer and Simon Biddle — both thinner than their lacrosse sticks. It was clear which would be the better team. Larry had picked all the big guys in the class. Some of them looked old enough to shave.

"We only have nine players," Itchy contested. "We're short-handed."

"All right, let's go!" Colonel R. barked, blasting on his whistle. "You know the rules. Choose your goalie, three defencemen, three attackers, and three midfielders."

"I only have nine players," Itchy whined again, but nobody seemed to listen. He dropped his hands in defeat and turned to his team, who stood clutching their lacrosse sticks in fear. "Who wants to play attacker?"

"I will." Boney stepped forward. He was the only one on his team who actually knew how to play the game.

Itchy lowered his voice. "You know what this means, don't you? It means you have to go head to head with prisoner 95."

"I know," Boney said.

"Let's go, ladies!" Colonel R. yelled. "Get out there and play!"

Larry's team assumed their positions as though they'd been playing lacrosse all their lives. Itchy's team milled about in confusion with no real plan of any kind.

"Move it!" Colonel R. shouted, stomping behind Itchy's players and blasting the whistle in their ears.

"Who's who?" Wormer asked, his skinny legs shaking.

"I don't know," Itchy answered. "But we'd better get out there before the Colonel has us for lunch."

"But where are we supposed to stand?" Biddle whimpered, his braces flashing.

"I don't know. Stand anywhere," Itchy said. "Just pick a man and stand opposite him. I'll play goal."

"We're doomed," Wormer said.

"Hold your sticks up," Boney advised them. "And whatever you do, don't let them hit you with the ball."

Itchy's team exchanged terrified looks.

Colonel R. blew the whistle. He pointed at Boney and Larry, motioning for them to squat in faceoff position. Placing the ball between their two sticks, he pursed his lips to blow the whistle again. But before the whistle sounded, Larry lunged at the ball, snatched it up with his stick, bashed Boney to the ground, ran toward Itchy, and immediately drove the ball full force at his head. Itchy went sprawling to the ground with a shriek of pain, the candy apple quarter his mother gave him fly-ing from his pocket.

Colonel R. waved his hands in the air, blasting his whistle wildly. "You have to wait for the signal!"

"You did that on purpose!" Boney yelled at Larry. He rushed to where Itchy lay on the ground. "Itchy . . . are you all right?" He slapped Itchy's face lightly, trying to revive his friend.

Itchy moaned. "What happened?"

"Walk it off, Red!" Colonel R. shouted.

Boney looked up at the gym teacher. "I think he's really hurt."

"Hey, look, a quarter!" Larry Harry said, scooping Itchy's quarter from the grass.

"That's my candy apple money!" Itchy cried.

"Get him outta here, Boneham!" Colonel R. ordered. "Take him to see the nurse."

NURSE CANE was far more understanding than Colonel R. She gave Itchy an aspirin and some ice for the lump on his head.

"Must be lacrosse season," she clucked, affixing a bandage over the lump.

"Actually, it's jerk season," Itchy moped. "That thief stole my money."

"You need to be more careful," the nurse admonished.

"It's not him that needs to be careful," Boney said. He sat on a small stool in one corner of the nurse's office, watching.

"Shouldn't you get back to class?" Nurse Cane asked.

"Oh . . . I'd better stay and make sure Itchy's okay," Boney said, not wanting to go back to face Larry Harry.

By the time the bell rang, Itchy's head was neatly bandaged and he was feeling well enough to hazard the walk home. But when they came out of Nurse Cane's office, Boney and Itchy found Squeak sitting on the top rung of the janitor's ladder outside the library, a "geek" sign pinned to his shirt. The rest of the students bustled by, enjoying their candy apples.

Itchy looked at the apples longingly as Boney helped Squeak down from the ladder.

"You have to stay out of their way," Boney told his friend, unpinning the sign from his shirt.

Squeak shrugged. "It really wasn't so bad. I was considering the dynamics of gravitation while I was sitting there. And I was thinking we should get a mascot for

the clubhouse. What happened to your head?" he asked
Itchy.

"Prisoner 95," Itchy grumbled. "And the worst part
is, he stole my candy apple money. Why do we need a
mascot?"

Just as he said this, Larry Harry shouted down the
hall. "Hey, Red! Have an apple on me!" he yelled, then
drove a candy apple at Itchy.

Itchy ducked his bandaged head but Boney caught
the apple easily with one hand. He was about to throw
it back when Itchy snatched it from him.

"Thanks," he said, unwrapping the apple.

"Lacrosse is a very dangerous game," Squeak
pointed out. "Lots of accidents can happen."

"It wasn't an accident," Itchy snarled, his mouth full
of candy apple.

Boney agreed. "The only thing really dangerous
about the game is playing against inmates like Larry
and his goons. Come on. Let's get out of here before
Larry launches any more apples."

Itchy raised his eyebrows hopefully, but Boney
pulled him from the school into the yard.

The boys walked across the school grounds and
along the street toward home, past the Super Quick
dry cleaners owned by Mr. Martini (who gave out

discount dry cleaning coupons for trick or treat that expired a week after Hallowe'en), and Top Drawer Insurance, with the expensive cars out front, past the Pets Plus shop that never seemed to have any pets for sale, and Zelda's, the women's clothing store with its unchanging display of faded hats and tired shoes. Itchy stopped when they reached the variety store on the corner, peering longingly through the window at the chocolate bars, his candy apple now a barren wooden stick in his hand.

"Why don't you just buy something?" Boney said.

Itchy looked at him mournfully. "I haven't got any money."

"Me neither," Boney said. "But my aunt bought more peanut butter and crackers."

"And my dad bought some giant jars of honey," Squeak added. "But no butter or bread."

"What are you supposed to do with giant jars of honey?" Boney asked.

Squeak shrugged. "I don't know. He said it was better for us than white sugar. He bought a lot of it."

Itchy rubbed his hands together. "Excellent. Just point me in the right direction."

BACK AT THE CLUBHOUSE, Itchy happily stuffed his face, swirling honey from a big spoon over his stack of crackers. Squeak scanned the horizon with his telescope.

"Every clubhouse has a mascot," he said.

"I'm not wearing some stupid suit," Itchy grunted through a mouthful of crackers.

Squeak sighed. "You don't have to wear a suit. Not all mascots are people in costume. They can be anything: even a goldfish, or a hamster or something."

"We don't own a hamster," Itchy said.

Boney listened silently to his friends' conversation, his brow furrowed in thought as he tugged on his chin with his fingers.

"You're gonna grow a beard if you keep that up," Itchy said, dribbling honey on another stack of crackers.

Boney leaned back in his chair. "We should go to the mill tonight to do some investigating," he announced.

Itchy stopped mid dribble. "Why?" He gestured at his stack of crackers. "We're so happy here. Why do you want to spoil things?"

Squeak collapsed his telescope in his hands, considering Boney's suggestion. "It would be a good idea to do a little sleuthing around. But I promised my dad I'd help him rewire the bathroom tonight. He found an old hand-dryer in the garbage and he wants to install it in the wall. He says it'll save us from having to wash a bunch of towels."

"And you can count me out," Itchy said, standing up from the table and furiously stuffing crackers in his mouth. "It's dinnertime."

Boney rolled his eyes. "Fine, I'll go myself, then."

Itchy shook his head. "Not safe," he mumbled.

"Yeah, well, it needs to be done," Boney snapped. "How are we going to know if our Apparator works if we don't find a ghost to test it on?"

Itchy pushed the rest of the crackers in his mouth before making his way to Escape Hatch #2. "Good luck," he said, then slid down the pole.

"You could wait until tomorrow night," Squeak offered. "I could go with you then." But he could tell by the look on Boney's face that he wasn't willing to wait. "Okay . . . well . . . have fun," Squeak said, and disappeared down the pole.

"William!" Boney's aunt shouted out the kitchen window. "Supper's ready!"

CHAPTER SIX

THE GHOST OF THE OLD MILL

"What is it?" Boney asked as his aunt heaped a pile of grey glop on his plate.

"*Supper Surprise.*"

Boney stared at his uncle across the table. His uncle raised his bushy eyebrows sympathetically. They sighed in unison, then lifted their forks and dutifully began to eat. When Boney had managed to choke down half his supper, he lowered his fork to the table and asked to be excused. His aunt eyed his half-finished plate critically.

"It was very good," Boney lied. "I just don't have much of an appetite tonight."

"It's all that candy you eat in that clubhouse of yours," his aunt complained as she cleared his plate from the table and slopped his leftovers back into the pot. "I'm sure your friend Squeak would love to have such a wholesome meal. His father hasn't got a clue in the kitchen, and it's not as if his mother is going to come traipsing back from whatever cabaret she's running around with."

"Mildred!" Boney's uncle exclaimed.

"Not to worry, though," his aunt continued. "It'll be hot and ready for supper tomorrow. It's supposed to be even better the second day."

"Yes, ma'am," Boney conceded. "I was thinking of going for a short bike ride, if that's okay."

His aunt peered out the kitchen window. "It's near dark."

"I'll stay on the sidewalk," Boney promised.

She cocked her head to one side. "Do you hear that buzzing?" she asked.

Boney didn't answer. Instead, he took the opportunity to slip out of the kitchen and into the garage to retrieve his bike. Boney's metallic-blue Schwinn stood at the ready. It had everything a boy like Boney could want: sparkly silver banana seat, chrome sissy-bar for transporting friends, and wide whitewall tires guaranteed to leave an impressive skid.

Boney wheeled his bike from the garage, the playing card he had clipped with a clothespin to the spokes clicking nicely. He hopped on the bike and pedalled down the driveway to the sidewalk. He waved to Squeak's dad, who was stepping out of his old brown Oldsmobile, hand-dryer in tow. Boney rode toward Itchy's, where his dad was just leaving for another show and his wife was kissing him at the door.

"Good luck, Mr. Schutz," Boney called out as he pedalled past.

Mr. Schutz curled his lip and struck a pose, pointing at Boney.

Itchy's dog, Snuff, streaked from beneath the porch and lunged at Boney's ankle, tearing at his pant leg. Boney kicked as best he could, his bike swerving dangerously on the sidewalk. Then Mrs. Pulmoni's cat appeared, running into the street, causing Snuff to abandon his attack on Boney and take up the chase. Mrs. Scheider's schnauzers joined the fray, barking furiously through their living-room window.

Boney pedalled to the end of the street, then rested, allowing the bike to coast as he enjoyed the regular *bump bump bump* of the tires over the cracks in the sidewalk. He veered to the left. The street rolled and twisted toward the river. Except for a few lonely houses, the road was dark with trees. The sun was fading quickly. There was a chill in the air. It was late September, after all.

Boney zipped along, punching in and out of the lamplight for several blocks until the streetlights disappeared altogether. He pedalled more slowly, squinting at the slender crescent of moon floating among the stars. He remembered what Squeak had said about the full moon and the ghost of the Old Mill. A shiver ran up his spine. He wished Itchy and Squeak were with him. But it didn't stop him from pushing on.

The whitewall tires on Boney's Schwinn whizzed over the pavement. Soon the street became little more than a rocky path. The bike tires bounced off stones, and Boney's sneakered feet flew from the pedals with the force. The path curved down to where the river slithered like a glittering snake at the bottom of the hill. And there, beside the river, were the ruins of the haunted mill.

Boney kicked back on the coaster brake, skidding to a stop in the dirt. Boulders from the crumbled walls gleamed like bones in the night. He listened intently, the sound of his own breathing rasping in his ears. He wondered if he should turn around and go home. He hesitated, then pushed off with one foot, and his bike wobbled forward. He would just take a peek, he told himself. He wouldn't stay long.

At the bottom of the hill, Boney dismounted. Now that he was closer, he could see the familiar shape of the mill ruins. It formed a giant horseshoe with three walls still standing, the fourth a heap of stones on the ground. The roof was missing entirely but the old water turbine was still intact, a motionless wooden wheel against the sky.

Boney leaned his bike on the rubble pile. Peering over the stones, he could see several rusty tin cans scattered inside the walls and a pit where fires had been built over the years. An old log had been dragged beside the fire for sitting. Bits of paper littered the ground, along with a few pieces of discarded clothing here and there. Nothing out of the ordinary, Boney reassured himself. Nothing *ghostly*.

All at once his eyes caught something glinting near the firepit, something he hadn't noticed right away. It twinkled invitingly, then faded, then twinkled again.

That's weird, Boney thought, staring at the twinkling thing.

He wondered if he shouldn't just leave, forget about the twinkling altogether, then decided it was his duty to investigate. Squeak and Itchy would have wanted him to. Well . . . Squeak, at least.

Climbing over the stones, Boney found himself standing within the old foundation walls of the mill. The air felt somehow colder. Boney shivered. He stepped cautiously toward the firepit. The mysterious object glimmered invitingly as he drew close. It was probably just a piece of glass, or an old length of wire, Boney told himself. Or perhaps it was a glass lens, held together with wire. As in wire glasses . . . left behind . . . by a kid . . . who was eaten by a ghost!

Boney gulped. Just a few feet more and he would have an answer.

As he approached the edge of the firepit, he heard a terrible sound—an awful, blood-curdling noise that seemed to rise from the stones along the wall in front of him. Boney froze, the hair bristling on the back of his neck, his heart pounding wildly in his chest. The ghost of the mill had come to kill him! It moaned again, even louder and more horrifying than before. Boney opened his mouth to scream as a white form shot out from behind the stone wall, streaking toward him.

Boney spun around, his sneakers pounding the dirt as he ran. Clearing the pile of stones in a single leap, he wrenched his bike from its resting spot and jumped onto the seat, legs pumping with all their might, stones spraying from his back tire. He crested the top of the hill in seconds, convinced the ghost was screaming after him. Careening along the road, he nearly drove right into Larry Harry walking with Jones and Jones.

"Where's the fire, Bonehead?" Larry yelled.

But Boney didn't even slow down. He tore past Larry Harry, nearly knocking him to the ground.

"Get back here, you little creep!" Larry shouted, but Boney was already a silhouette on the horizon.

Boney streaked along the sidewalk toward home. Turning into the driveway, he practically slammed his bike into the garage as he skidded to a halt. Jumping off, he threw open the door and rolled his bike to its place along the back wall. He didn't bother to engage the kickstand but simply dropped the bike and ran, slamming the door behind him. He rushed into the house, through the kitchen, past his aunt and uncle, who stared at him in surprise, and all the way up to his room, shutting the door with a bang. He breathlessly pulled the towel from the Tele-tube and placed the tube to his lips.

"Squeak, are you there? Over."

Silence. Boney brushed the hair from his eyes in agitation. "Come in, Squeak, it's urgent—over."

More silence. Boney dropped the Tele-tube and paced around his bedroom, hands on his hips. He was just about to storm over to his friend's house when he heard the familiar sound of Squeak's voice floating through the tube.

"Squeak here."

Boney rushed to the tube, speaking frantically. "I saw it!"

"Saw what?"

"The ghost!"

There was silence on the other end of the tube. "You mean . . . the one at the haunted mill?"

"Yes! *The* ghost!" Boney shouted.

"Are you sure?"

"It chased me."

Loud rustling emanted from Squeak's Tele-tube.

"Itchy wants to know what's going on."

"Tell him I saw the ghost and we need to expedite the Apparator. Tell him we have to go to school early tomorrow so we can register our entry in the Invention Convention right away."

Boney heard murmuring through the tube, then a long pause.

"He's freaking out," Squeak finally reported.

"Tell him he's not backing out of this—it's too scientifically important! We need to field test our invention. I don't care how scared he is!"

"What did the ghost look like?" Squeak asked. But before Boney could answer, there was a confusion of footsteps in the hall outside his bedroom door.

"William . . . what's going on?" his aunt called out. "It's past your bedtime."

"Gotta go!" Boney hissed into the tube. "Just tell him to be up and ready early tomorrow morning—or else."

He covered the tube with the towel then quickly

changed into his pyjamas and climbed into bed. Reaching to turn off his bedside lamp, he got a flash of the ghost in his head and decided to sleep with the light on instead.

CHAPTER SEVEN

A Plan for Revenge

The next morning, Boney left the house early to collect his friends. The second he reached Squeak's walkway, he was hit in the head with a rolled up newspaper.

"Hey, watch it!" Boney shouted, picking up the paper and tossing it back at the paperboy, who whizzed down the street on his bike.

Boney reached to ring the bell on Squeak's house just as the door opened.

"I finished the schematics for the Apparator," Squeak said, stepping onto the porch and closing the door behind him. He produced a long scroll from his bag, unrolling it so Boney could see. "I'm only missing one thing — the rare earth magnets. But I've ordered them through the mail, so we should have them in a week or so."

"Excellent job," Boney said, admiring Squeak's drawing. "We can start work on it tonight."

Squeak carefully replaced the drawing in his bag as they walked to Itchy's house. When they arrived, Snuff leapt from the porch, chasing after a squirrel. Boney shook his head as he rang the doorbell. "How can you think he's cute?"

Squeak and Boney waited at the door for several minutes. Boney was about to ring the bell again when Mr. Schutz answered the door, still wearing his Elvis costume.

"More fans," he muttered. "I gotta get a security guard . . . or something."

Mrs. Schutz appeared beside him in her purple bathrobe. She handed her husband a thick sandwich. He held the sandwich in the air for the boys to see.

"Peanut butter and banana," he announced. "Breakfast of Kings." He took a big bite of the sandwich then turned and walked to the bottom of the stairs. "Itchy!" he yelled.

Mrs. Schutz smiled. "You're up early this morning," she said to Boney and Squeak. "Something special going on?"

Boney smiled politely back. "Science stuff."

Itchy finally appeared, his hair messier than usual, a blueberry muffin in each hand. He promptly stuffed a muffin in his mouth, swallowed, then immediately devoured the second one. His mom handed him a brown lunch bag and kissed him as he walked out the door.

"Why are we up so early?" He opened his lunch bag and began eating his sandwich.

"We need to enter our submission forms for the convention," Boney said. "And I want to talk about our plan for revenge."

Itchy stopped mid-bite. "What do you mean, *plan for revenge?* I thought we were talking about the convention. You never said anything about a plan for revenge."

"Yes, I did. I told you I was hatching something. Anyway, don't worry about it. It's a good plan. You're going to like it."

Itchy swallowed a big bite of sandwich. "Shouldn't we stick to one crazy idea at a time?"

"You don't even know what it is yet."

"Yeah, but I'm getting indigestion just thinking about it."

"Maybe you should chew your food better," Squeak advised.

Itchy stopped dead in his tracks, his eyes widening. "Guys . . . we forgot, there's football practice today."

"So what?" Boney said. "We're not on the team."

"Yeah . . . but *they* are." Itchy pointed his half-eaten

sandwich down the street to where Larry Harry and Jones and Jones were approaching.

"Don't they ever sleep?" Squeak said. "Why don't they go steal some mail and leave us alone?"

Itchy suddenly bolted, running toward the school, frantically stuffing his sandwich in his mouth. Larry Harry and Jones and Jones took up the chase.

"But it's too early to go in yet," Squeak said, running alongside Itchy.

Itchy ran faster. "Who cares? I'd rather sit in the office than face that criminal this early in the morning."

Boney caught up to his friends. "I promise, after my plan is enacted, we'll never have to run from those creeps again."

"If we survive that long," Itchy wailed, yanking on the door to the school.

The Odds clattered up the stairs, bursting breathlessly into Mr. Harvey's science lab. Mr. Harvey looked up in surprise from his desk.

"Whoa, whoa, whoa! Where's the fire, boys?"

"Sorry, Mr. Harvey," Boney said. "We're just excited about our invention for the convention."

"Yeah," Itchy said, looking nervously over his shoulder as Larry Harry cruised menacingly by the classroom door.

Mr. Harvey pulled an entry form from his desk and

handed it to the boys. "I'll be interested to see what you come up with this year."

"Oh, I believe you'll be impressed," Squeak said as he pulled a pen from his breast pocket and began to fill out the form.

"That's doubtful," a voice said behind them.

The Odds turned to see Edward Wormer sitting at the back of the class, filling out a form. He clicked his pen shut, then rose from his seat and strolled over to where the boys were standing. He shot a glance over Squeak's shoulder.

"The *Apparator*," he read aloud. "Is that a typo?"

Squeak spun around, whipping the form behind his back. "All entries are confidential until the day of the convention. You know the rules."

Wormer raised his eyebrows smugly as he folded his entry form and handed it to Mr. Harvey. "And winner takes all," he said. "I already know what I'm going to buy with the prize money."

"Oh, yeah?" Itchy said. "So do we!"

"Great," Wormer said. "You can help deliver it to my house, then." He glided confidently from the classroom, the Odds squinting angrily at him as he left.

"He's not going to win," Squeak vowed as he quickly filled in the rest of the form and handed it to Mr. Harvey.

"Who cares?" Itchy said, peering into the hall where Larry Harry and Jones and Jones stood. "We're going to get killed anyway."

"They've got football practice," Boney reminded him.

"Yeah, but we've got gym first thing this morning," Itchy whined.

Squeak looked at his watch. "Well, at least we've got time to review the schematics for the Apparator before class." He looked at Mr. Harvey. "Is it okay if we use the science lab?"

Mr. Harvey agreed and the boys bustled to the back of the class. They pored over Squeak's drawing until the bell rang, calling them to homeroom.

The boys took their seats. Miss Sours was already glowering overtop her glasses.

"I didn't get a chance to outline my plan for revenge," Boney complained, leaning toward Itchy and whispering in his quietest voice.

"Mr. Boneham!" Miss Sours shrieked, smacking her yardstick across her desk.

Larry Harry grinned menacingly from across the room, smacking his fist in the palm of his hand.

"I'll tell you in gym," Boney murmured from the corner of his mouth.

As usual, Miss Sours walked up and down the aisles, monitoring the students while the announcements were read over the loudspeaker, the class jumping with relief from their seats when the bell rang and hustling from the room. Except the Odds, who lingered cautiously at the back of the class, afraid Larry Harry and the evil twins were waiting for them in the hall.

"Is there a problem, Mr. Boneham?" Miss Sours sniffed.

"No, ma'am."

"Then get to class!"

The Odds huddled together as they moved down the hall toward the gym lockers. When they reached the end of the hall, Squeak ducked into the library, waving sympathetically to his friends.

"Be careful," he said.

Boney and Itchy continued along the hall and down the stairs to the change room. Thankfully, it was empty. Larry Harry and all the other boys were already changed and heading toward the lacrosse field.

"At least I have a decent shirt to wear today," Itchy said, pulling on a lime-green T-shirt.

Boney raised his eyebrows skeptically but said nothing while he changed into his gym clothes. He placed his arm around Itchy's shoulders as they left the school for the playing field. "Now, here's my plan for revenge."

"MOVE IT, PEOPLE!" Colonel R. shouted, blasting on his whistle from centre field. "Same teams as yesterday!"

Itchy and Boney joined the group of skinny misfits milling around the bench.

"I have to fall out of what?" Itchy said, staring at Boney in horror.

"The tree," Boney said. "But you don't fall. You fly out of the tree like a screaming demon."

"Oh, *that's* better," Itchy derided. "For a minute there I thought I had to fall out of a tree. I'm not doing it. It's too dangerous."

"The lowest branch is only ten feet up," Boney said. "Besides, I'm rigging up a harness system controlled by a rope. We'll wrap it around the branch and I'll work the rope so you won't get hurt."

"Why can't *you* wear the harness and *I* control the rope?" Itchy asked.

"Because I'm the bait," Boney said. "I'm going to lure them in." He made a motion with his hands as though luring a fish with a rod and reel.

Itchy stared at his friend in disgust. "Why doesn't Squeak lure them in?"

"Because I'm the fastest runner. They'll chase me, I'll run back, then work the rope."

Colonel R. blew his whistle. "Take your positions!"

Larry Harry's team ran onto the field, swinging their

lacrosse sticks threateningly. The misfits bumped into each other, shoving and arguing over who was playing what position.

"I don't like it," Itchy complained, jogging next to Boney.

"You can't chicken out this time," Boney said. "Don't you want to get those criminals back for what they've done to us? It's a great plan! They'll pee their pants and die when they see you streaking out of that tree."

" . . . I don't know . . ." Itchy said.

"Get a move on!" Colonel R. screamed, his whistle piercing the air. He pointed at Itchy and Larry, indicating the start of the game, then blew his whistle again as he dropped the ball.

Larry dove, scooping up the ball and driving it right at Itchy, hitting him square in the stomach. Itchy doubled over and collapsed. Boney rushed to his friend and helped him to his feet.

"Do you want to be a human target for the rest of your life?" he asked as they limped across the field to the nurse's office.

Itchy slumped against Boney's shoulder. "Fine," he said, gritting his teeth in pain. "I'll do it."

CHAPTER EIGHT

ZOMBIE ELVIS

Later that week, the boys convened at the clubhouse.

"I don't have any white sheets," Itchy reported to his friends, his disembodied head poking through the hole in Escape Hatch #1. "But I found an old tire and a camera." He plunked a Polaroid Swing camera onto the clubhouse floor. "It has film in it and everything. I left the tire at the base of the tree. It's too heavy to carry up the ladder."

"Hey! I lent you that camera months ago," Squeak said, snatching up the Polaroid and checking it for damage. "What are we supposed to do with an old tire?"

"We can hang it from a rope," Itchy said, climbing into the clubhouse.

Boney and Squeak stared in bewilderment at Itchy's popsicle-pink T-shirt.

"My mom dyed all the white sheets pink to suit

her most recent decor decision," Itchy explained. "She dyed the towels and all our underwear by mistake, too. The whole house is just one big bubble-gum-pink nightmare."

Squeak furrowed his brow with concern. "Why would we hang a tire from the clubhouse?"

"To swing on," Itchy said. He held up a length of rope.

Boney rolled his eyes. "I asked you to do *one* simple thing," he said. "We need you to dress in white for our revenge plan." He turned to Squeak. "What about you, Squeak? Do you have any white sheets at your place?"

Squeak shook his head. "Dad and I use sleeping bags. It's for the best, really, because I can't imagine what the sheets would look like if Dad were responsible for washing them."

"Well, we can't have a pink ghost," Boney said.

"What do you mean, ghost?" Itchy jumped in. "You said there weren't any ghosts of any kind in this plan."

"Not any real ones," Boney replied. "Just fake ghosts."

"You said I could be a zombie."

"Right. You're a zombie. But we still need a white sheet."

"Why don't *you* provide the white sheet, seeing as this whole zombie thing is your idea?" Itchy demanded.

Boney sighed. "You know my aunt only buys red-and-black plaid flannel sheets. She read somewhere that they repel bugs."

"Well, that's that, then," Itchy said with a measure of relief. "Guess the plan is off."

Squeak squinted from behind his goggles. "Where'd your aunt read that?"

"Some women's magazine. Come on, Itchy," Boney pleaded. "There must be something you can wear. Go back home and look harder."

"I'm telling you, we don't have anything!" Itchy shouted.

"Try again!" Boney insisted. "I ran around collecting everything else." He pointed toward a pile of stuff to one side of the clubhouse: a length of webbing, a silver bucket, two flashlights, an old hockey helmet, a spotlight, and a feather pillow.

"And I brought all my special-effects materials," Squeak said. "Foam latex, silicone prosthetics, makeup, hair pomade, gelatin, wigs, false teeth—a creepy eye." Squeak held this up to his face, the eyeball bouncing lazily on the end of a spring. "I even received my blood capsules in the mail today." He produced a small cellophane bag filled with little capsules and sniffed it. "Smells like revenge to me."

Itchy took the bag from Squeak. "How do they work?"

Squeak opened the bag and popped a capsule in his mouth. "You just put them in your mouth like this . . . and when you're ready, bite down like a great white shark." He clamped down on the capsule and the fake blood spurted between the gap in his teeth.

"Cool," Itchy said.

"See?" Boney enthused. "We're going to dress you like a zombie-ghost kinda thing and send you flying out of the tree with blood and all kinds of horrible stuff. When Larry gets a look at you, he's going to cry like a baby for his mother. And we'll have the photos to prove it." He held the Polaroid in the air.

"And when they're begging for mercy, I'm going to tar and feather them—just like in medieval times," Squeak added, gesturing to the silver pail.

"Where are we going to get tar?" Itchy asked.

"Well, we can't use real tar," Squeak confessed. "But I thought of something just as good." He pulled a large jar of honey from his messenger bag. "If we dilute this by 20 percent with H_2O, it should have the desired viscosity. It'll take them weeks to wash this honey from their hair."

"This could be awesome," Itchy said.

"It *will* be awesome," Boney encouraged him. "So

all we need now is something white for you to wear. I'm sure there's something at your house. Come on. Squeak and I will help you look."

OVER AT ITCHY'S HOUSE, Itchy opened the linen cupboard door, revealing a stack of pink sheets and towels.

"See?" he said. "Everything's pink. There's not a white thing in the house."

Boney frowned at the pink sheets, his eyes drifting over to the open closet at the end of the hall. "What about that?" He pointed to Itchy's father's gleaming white Elvis costume.

"Oh, no," Itchy protested. "Forget it."

"It's perfect," Boney said, walking over and lifting the plastic covering from the suit.

"Ahhhh! Don't touch it!" Itchy slapped Boney's hand away. "That's my dad's spare. Nobody touches his costumes."

"Can't you just see it, Squeak?" Boney murmured, his eyes glazed with a trance-like ecstasy. "This costume will be perfect . . ."

"Those sequins would create quite an effect in the right light," Squeak agreed. "And those flared cuffs and sleeves will flap brilliantly as he's flying out of the tree like a . . . like a . . ." Squeak's voice trailed off as he searched for the right word.

"Like a screaming zombie Elvis," Boney said.

Itchy threw his hands in the air. "Am I the only one who isn't crazy here? I don't think you understand. If anything happens to that costume, I'm dead." He yanked the plastic back down over the suit.

"But you said it's his spare," Boney said, removing the costume from the rod. "We have to do it."

"No," Itchy refused.

"Just imagine how amazing it'll be . . ."

"You're out of your mind."

"It's brilliant!"

"Can't we just build the Apparator instead?" Itchy pleaded. He watched helplessly as Boney drifted down the hall with the costume. "I'm so doomed . . ."

UP IN THE CLUBHOUSE, Itchy folded his sparkling arms across his chest as Boney tightened the waistband on the costume with some safety pins. Squeak fussed with Itchy's makeup, adding the finishing touches to Zombie Elvis. You could hardly recognize Itchy, he looked so different. His hair was jet-black and slick with pomade. He had sideburns pencilled to the corners of his twisted blue mouth. One eye dangled horribly from the socket, while the other was distorted and sunken. His face was powdered a ghastly white and his hands were covered in horrible Frankenstein scars.

"We'd better not get this suit dirty," Itchy slurred for the umpteenth time through false teeth. "And I have to have it back before midnight. My dad checks in on it like a prison warden."

"No problem," Boney said. "The whole plan shouldn't take more than half an hour. But we'd better get ready. Larry and his fellow convicts will be walking home after soccer practice soon."

"At least I got to eat supper before I die," Itchy sulked. "And it was good, too. Tuna casserole. Not like that canned-soup stuff your aunt makes."

"I believe canned mushroom soup is one of the main ingredients in tuna casserole," Squeak corrected him.

"Well, it was good anyway," Itchy said. "My mom's a great cook. I'm going to miss all those delicious meals when I'm dead."

Boney laughed dismissively. "You're not going to die."

Itchy stared at him suspiciously with his one good eye, the other bouncing lightly on its spring. "Easy for you to say."

"Open wide," Squeak ordered, popping several fake

blood capsules into Itchy's mouth. "Okay, you know how it works. At the right moment, bite down hard on the capsules and then spit the blood all over—making sure not to get any on the suit, of course."

Itchy-Elvis nodded his head, the fake eye bouncing.

Squeak stood back, proudly admiring his work. "You'd make a great mascot," he said. "Zombie Elvis—I don't think any other club has such an innovative side-kick."

"Forget it," Itchy said.

"Too bad," Squeak sighed. He turned to Boney and saluted. "He's ready for the harness, Chief."

Boney produced the webbing harness and fitted it carefully around Itchy's thin frame.

"Are you sure this thing will hold?" Itchy mumbled warily, trying not to burst the blood capsule between his teeth.

"Sure it'll hold," Boney answered confidently. "I learned how to tie a harness in Scouts, remember?"

"That was a long time ago," Itchy reminded him.

"Well, it's kind of like riding a bike," Boney said, cheerfully. "You never really forget how to do it." He studied the harness for a moment. "Now where does this piece go?" he mused, holding up a loose end of rope.

"You said you knew what you were doing," Itchy grumbled.

"Don't worry. I was just kidding. See, it goes here." He pushed the end of the webbing through a small loop at the back of the harness and secured it, tugging on the harness to show how strong it was. Itchy tugged on it as well. While he was doing this, Boney squeezed his old hockey helmet over Itchy's blackened hair. "For extra protection."

"Ahhhh," Itchy wailed. "You're ripping my hair out!"

"Sorry." Boney adjusted the straps on the hockey helmet to fit Itchy's head. Then he produced a black magic marker and a large scribble pad with a diagram of the neighbouring streets. "Okay, listen up." He began drawing on the diagram, the way Colonel R. sometimes did on the chalkboard in gym class. "Here's the soccer field," he said, marking the spot on the pad with a big black "X." "Prisoner 95 and his henchmen will finish soccer practice at 8:00. At approximately 8:15 they'll stop to change their shoes at the bleachers, then walk down Bleaker Street to Joe's Variety on the eight corners to purchase soda and licorice. By 8:25, they'll be moving along Friendship to Van Avenue, where they'll cut across the street to the alley between Walker and Johnston. They'll reach Green Bottle at 8:33, where they'll deposit their soda cans in Mrs. Scheider's garbage can. They'll stop for two to three minutes to tease her schnauzers, then throw a few rocks at Mrs. Pulmoni's cat. That's when I step out from behind the mailbox into the streetlight. As soon as I see them, I'll give two sharp whistles." Boney demonstrated, giving two loud blasts with his fingers to his lips. "When they start to chase me, I'll signal Squeak with the flashlight," he signalled with the flashlight, "and run back to the clubhouse to man the rope. Squeak, the second they run under the south branch, you hit them with the honey. When they're rubbing their eyes, blind them with the spotlight. Itchy, that's your cue to come flying out of the tree, spitting blood and swinging the feather pillow. They won't know what hit them! Any questions?"

Itchy raised his hand. "What if I have to go to the bathroom?"

"Do you have to go to the bathroom?" Boney asked.

"No. But what if I do?"

"Then hold it until the manoeuvre is over."

Boney helped Itchy through the clubhouse window onto the big east branch of the clubhouse tree. Itchy inched along the branch to his position, trying not to catch the pants of his father's Elvis costume on the bark of the tree. He steadied himself to keep from falling as Squeak leaned out the window and handed him the feather pillow.

"Hold this end up," Squeak instructed. "I've loosened the stitches so the feathers will explode when you swing it."

Itchy nodded. He looked at Boney. "This had better work," he threatened.

"Don't worry," Boney assured him again. "It'll scare them senseless. When I give you the signal, you push off the branch, start swinging the pillow and spitting blood. I'll be down on the ground working the rope so you don't fall. Got it?"

Itchy-Elvis nodded.

"Ready with the tar and spotlight?"

Squeak saluted. "Ready, Chief."

"All right," Boney said. "I'm going down the street to wait for Larry Harry and the evil twins. Remember the code."

"Two sharp whistles," Squeak answered obediently.

"Right," Boney said. "As soon as you hear those whistles you'll know I've spotted them. When they start to chase me, I'll signal with the flashlight to Squeak. Squeak gives Itchy the signal to get ready," Boney made a slashing motion with his hand in Itchy's direction, "and it's showtime! Any final questions?"

The boys shook their heads.

"Good. I'm off. Good luck, men." Boney saluted his friends.

Squeak saluted back. Itchy-Elvis raised his hand to salute but almost slipped from the tree in the process and decided to just nod instead.

Boney slid down the pole to the ground. He skulked along the length of the house, hiding behind bushes and making his way to the street, trying to avoid the prying eyes of his nosy neighbours. Ducking out of the street-lamp light, he scurried behind Squeak's father's car. From this vantage point, he could see Itchy's mother sitting in a chair on her porch at 27 Green Bottle. He would have to take evasive measures. Crouching low, he slipped alongside the car into the street and shuffled quickly past Itchy's house, hiding behind Mrs. Pulmoni's old station wagon. But as he did this he was ambushed by Itchy's terrier, Snuff, who came snarling out from behind some garbage cans and grabbed the cuff of Boney's pants with his needle-sharp teeth.

"Get off me, you stupid mutt!" Boney growled hoarsely, struggling to pull his leg clear of the dog. But when he jerked his leg back, he lost his balance and tumbled into the street from behind the car, with the dog snapping and pulling on his pant leg.

"Is that you, Boney?" Itchy's mother called from the porch.

Boney waved back as though nothing was wrong, still trying to pull his leg free. Snuff snarled and tugged even harder. Several lights snapped on along the street.

"Oh, dear!" Itchy's mother cried once she'd realized

what all the confusion was about. "Snuff! You stop that this instant! Bad dog! Bad dog!" And then she gave two sharp whistles. "Come here right now!"

Boney wrestled with Snuff, trying to step over the dog and wrench himself free. Kicking and struggling, he tripped over his pant leg and fell to the ground, hitting the concrete. The flashlight bounced from his hands and blinked twice before rolling to the centre of the street, where it was instantly crushed by a passing car.

"Get outta the road, kid!" the driver barked as he drove by.

Boney looked at the crushed flashlight with dismay. He tried to pull himself upright, but Snuff still clung to his pant cuff, growling and snarling. "Go on!" Boney shouted, giving him a quick kick and sending the dog skittering backwards to the curb.

"I'll get his doggie treats," Itchy's mother called out, running into the house.

Snuff geared up and rushed again, but this time Boney stepped quickly out of the way and began running back to the clubhouse to warn the other Odd Fellows that the falling flashlight was not the official signal. He raced back to the tree, arms waving, Snuff barking and growling behind him.

"I said GO ON!" Boney screamed at the dog as he hit the old rubber tire at the base of the tree, stumbling wildly. He flailed to the ground and was suddenly splashed by a cold shower of sticky honey water. The spotlight blasted on. The Polaroid flashed. There was a horrible shriek followed by a thud as Itchy-Elvis leaped from the tree, feathers exploding everywhere. The blood capsules burst, gushing red goop from Itchy's mouth as his chin hit the ground, the special-effects eye popping from its socket and rolling into the dirt. The Polaroid whirred and a picture appeared from the camera, the image of Itchy in mid-flight slowly coming into focus. The light at the side of the house turned on and there stood Boney's aunt and uncle, with looks of shock and horror on their faces as the feathers from the exploded pillow floated gracefully down, adhering to Boney's honey-covered clothing. The whole mess was high-lighted like a vaudeville show by the spotlight, still faithfully manned by Squeak.

"That stupid old tire," Boney moaned from the ground.

Boney's aunt took one look at Itchy and fainted. Itchy's mother could be heard calling for Snuff down the street.

"Is . . . is that his eye?" Boney's uncle asked, pointing to the fake eye in the mud.

Boney retrieved the eye from the ground. "It's okay. It's only a fake."

He held the dripping eye in the air, the eyeball bouncing on the end of its spring. His aunt fluttered awake, took one look at the eye, and fainted again.

"Come, now, Mildred, it's only a fake," his uncle tried to console her, tapping lightly on her hand. He turned to Boney. "You'd better clean this up quickly and hope your aunt doesn't remember a thing after she wakes up." He gathered his wife and took her inside.

Boney pushed the eye into his pants pocket and leaned over to see if his friend was all right. He shook Itchy's arm.

"Itchy . . . are you okay?"

Snuff trotted up to his master and began licking the fake blood from his mouth and cheeks.

"Snuff, cookies!" Itchy's mother called from the street.

The dog tore from the yard, racing to get his treat.

Itchy groaned, his eyes blinking. "What happened?" he asked, raising his head shakily. He looked up at the feather-covered Boney. The spotlight streaming behind him made him look like an angelic chicken. "Am I dead?" he gulped.

"You jumped too soon," Boney-Chicken explained. "The flashlight was a false alarm. And I tripped over your old tire." He helped Itchy to his feet.

"Oh no," Itchy said, looking at the blood-stained Elvis outfit. "My dad's going to kill me."

"We'll get it dry cleaned," Boney said, supporting Itchy around the waist. "Squeak — douse the light."

Squeak turned off the spotlight, then slipped down the escape pole to where Boney and Itchy stood.

"My dad's going to kill me," Itchy moaned again, looking at the red-stained suit.

"I'm pretty sure those blood capsules are water soluble," Squeak said, handing Itchy the Polaroid snapshot. "It's a good picture . . . if that's any consolation . . ."

"We'll have the Elvis costume cleaned and back in the closet before your dad notices it's gone," Boney said.

Itchy just shook his head. "Bad idea," he mumbled. "I knew it was a bad idea from the beginning." He crumpled the snapshot in his hand.

CHAPTER NINE

A King-Sized Mess

Boney and Squeak helped Itchy into Boney's house and sat him on a chair in the kitchen. Boney unfastened the strap on the hockey helmet and worked it off Itchy's head. They could hear Boney's aunt wailing hysterically from her bedroom upstairs, and Boney's uncle softly consoling her.

"Wait here," Boney told Itchy. "I'll get you some clean clothes from upstairs."

Boney reappeared moments later with a bundle of clothes from his bedroom. He handed them to Itchy, then guided him to the bathroom off the kitchen. When Itchy reappeared he was wearing one of Boney's old Superman T-shirts and a pair of his faded old jeans. His face was newly scrubbed, but there was still a light stain on his cheek where the fake blood had been.

"At least it's better than the shirt Squeak lent me," he said. He surveyed the ruined suit, his face crumpling in anguish. "I may as well just run away and join the circus."

"It'll be okay," Boney reassured him. "We'll take it to Mr. Martini's cleaners. He's open late on Thursday nights."

Itchy looked up, a spark of hope glimmering in his eye then fading again at the sight of the blood-stained costume. He shook his head, burying his face in his hands. "I'm done. This is a disaster."

"It's going to be okay," Boney insisted. "I promise."

"That's what I was afraid of," Itchy groaned into his hands. "As soon as you start making promises, everything goes horribly wrong."

Boney ignored his friend. "It won't take more than an hour."

"You're not going anywhere," his uncle said, appearing suddenly in the kitchen and trying to look stern. "Your aunt is upstairs with a sick headache. Go home, boys. Boney is grounded for the rest of his life. Do you understand?" he said, raising his voice so his wife would hear. "The rest of his life!"

The boys rose obediently.

"But Uncle!" Boney protested.

"Please, Boney, not another word," his uncle said as Itchy and Squeak slunk out of the house, the screen door slapping lightly behind them. "I want you to . . . uh . . .

clean yourself up then go to your room and think about what you've done."

Boney dragged the dirty costume up the stairs to his room. He threw the costume on his bed, and slumped down beside it. Grounded for life? It seemed like a harsh punishment given the circumstances. After all, no one got really hurt.

Boney moped for a while, then found some clean clothes and shuffled across the hall to the shower. There was so much honey, and so many feathers in his hair, he needed half a bottle of shampoo just to get it clean. What's more, he had to keep unclogging the feathers from the shower drain.

When Boney returned to his room, Squeak's voice drifted over the Tele-tube. "Is anybody there?"

Boney removed the towel and pressed the tube to his lips. "We really messed up this time."

"It was simply a malfunction," Squeak consoled. "The plan was a good one . . . if it had turned out the way we imagined."

"We didn't get revenge on Larry Harry. The whole thing was just a big failure."

"There's still the Invention Convention and the ghost at the mill."

"I'm grounded for life," Boney said.

"You've been grounded for life before," Squeak reminded him.

"My aunt fainted twice."

"She fainted three times over the parachute caper."

"True . . ."

"What are we going to do about Itchy's dad's costume?" Squeak asked.

Boney leaned his chin in his hand. "I have to get it to Mr. Martini's or Itchy will never speak to me again. If he hadn't left that stupid old tire at the bottom of the tree, things might have ended better."

"Uh, yeah . . ."

"Anyway, I'm going to wait until my aunt and uncle are asleep, then sneak out and bike the costume over to the cleaners."

There was a pause as Squeak considered Boney's new plan. "Do you think that's a good idea?"

"It's our only hope. If Itchy's dad comes home from his show and finds his spare Elvis costume missing, Itchy is going to run away and join the circus."

"It's too bad we don't have a robot," Squeak said. "We could send it to the cleaners with the Elvis costume instead. That way, nobody would get in trouble."

"Yeah."

"Well," Squeak sighed, "joining the circus might not

be so bad. Itchy likes animals. At least, he's always eating animal crackers in class . . ."

There was a sudden flurry of footsteps outside the bedroom door.

"Got to go!" Boney whispered, throwing the towel over the Tele-tube and leaping into bed. He turned off the light and shut his eyes as though asleep.

The door to his room flew open. His uncle stood frowning in the doorway, his long shadow stretching across the floor. He surveyed the room, then closed the door with a click.

BONEY WAITED until he was sure his aunt and uncle were asleep before slipping from bed. He pushed his feet into his sneakers then crept across the room. Opening the door a tiny crack, he shut it just as quickly. His uncle had fallen asleep on the couch watching TV. He could see him from the top of the stairs.

Boney checked the alarm clock beside his bed. It was after ten o'clock. Itchy's father was due home at midnight. That left less than two hours to get the costume to the cleaners and return it. Boney scratched his head. He had to get out. But how?

He eyed the window, where the Tele-tube lay concealed beneath the towel. He would have to get out that way, he decided. There was no other choice with his uncle sleeping on the couch in the living room.

Boney uncovered the Tele-tube. "Squeak, are you there?" he whispered.

There was a soft rustling at the other end of the line.

"I'm here," Squeak's sleepy voice answered.

"There's a slight glitch in the plan," Boney reported. "Uncle is snoring on the couch. I'm going to Plan B."

"What's Plan B?" Squeak asked.

"Operation Window."

"As in . . . *climbing* out the window?"

"Roger that."

"I'm not sure I like the smell of this," Squeak said. "It sounds very prickly."

"It's not prickly at all," Boney countered. "I have to save Itchy from the circus."

"It seems rather drastic. Our windows are quite a ways up."

"It's getting late," Boney said. "I have no choice."

"Boney . . ." Squeak's cautious voice filtered through the tube. "Be careful."

CHAPTER TEN

SAVING ITCHY FROM THE CIRCUS

Boney pulled a sweater over his T-shirt, emptied his piggy bank into his pockets, filled his Triple-X Turbo Blaster water gun that he'd got for his birthday the year before with water from the large glass next to his bed, folded the stained Elvis costume into a pillowcase, and unlocked the window. Raising the sash slowly, Boney was careful not to disconnect the Tele-tube from its housing in the frame.

He stuck one leg over the sill, dangling it tentatively over the ledge. He paused, gathering his courage. The air felt cool against his skin. Bending forward, he pushed his head and shoulders through the opening. Squeak's worried face peered back at him from across the divide that separated their two houses. He pointed down with concern.

Boney looked down. The ground seemed a lot farther away at night than it did in the daylight. But he couldn't turn back now. He gave Squeak the thumbs-up, at the same time measuring with his foot the distance to the trellis that supported his aunt's precious climbing roses. Lowering himself down, his sneakered foot probed for a foothold, the thorns of the roses scratching and clawing at his leg. When at last he found his footing, Boney grabbed the wooden trellis and lowered himself out the window.

Moving slowly, Blaster in one hand, pillowcase in the other, Boney desperately tried to avoid the sharp claws of the roses. They pulled at his pants and his shirt, tearing at the fabric. More than once, he had to stifle a cry as a thorn pierced his hand. "I hate roses," he cursed through clenched teeth as he picked his way down to the living-room window. Looking through, he could see his uncle sleeping on the couch, his chest rising and falling, his moustache billowing in and out with each breath. Boney ducked out of sight as his uncle snorted and jumped, rolling like an old walrus onto his side.

When he was sure it was safe, Boney continued his descent. Everything was working beautifully. He was just about to congratulate himself on his stealth when the pillowcase containing the stained costume caught on a big thorn. Boney tugged. The pillowcase wouldn't budge. He tugged again. Still nothing. Then he yanked, and the pillowcase ripped along its seam, sending Boney crashing in a heap to the ground, the Triple-X water blaster bouncing from his hand, the wind knocked with a loud grunt from his lungs. He lay there in agony, terrified to move lest his uncle appear.

Squeak's window rattled open. "Are you okay?" he whispered down.

"I'm fine," Boney answered, rubbing his ankle. He waved Squeak off, retrieved the water gun and pillowcase, and pulled himself to his feet, making his way across the lawn to the garage.

Inside the garage, Boney knelt down, removing the playing card and clothespin he kept pegged to the spokes of his bike. Normally, he liked the noise the card made, but tonight, silence was essential. Setting the card and pin aside, he grabbed the pillowcase and wheeled his bike noiselessly from the garage. Just to be safe, he walked the bike to the street before slinging his leg over the crossbar and pushing off.

As he pedalled past Itchy's house, he heard the familiar sound of Snuff's nails scrabbling down the concrete walkway in pursuit. Snuff raced up to the bike, but before he could attack, Boney aimed the Blaster gun and hosed the dog in the face, sending Snuff skittering with a yelp back to the porch.

Boney pedalled faster, tucking the gun in the pillow-case, the pillowcase bumping wildly against his knee. When he reached the cleaners, he skidded to a stop and rested his bike against the wall of the building.

The door jangled loudly as Boney entered the store, the smell of chemicals and scorched cloth jumping into his nose. Mr. Martini stood like an undertaker behind the counter, a thin, grey-haired wisp of a man with thick, black-framed glasses even bigger than Squeak's goggles. Boney thumped the pillowcase onto the counter

"I need this outfit cleaned right away."

Mr. Martini slowly extracted the blaster gun and the Elvis suit. He placed the pistol to one side with a questioning look, then began carefully poring over the blood stains with his thick lenses. He fished a magnifying glass out from behind the counter and continued to study the stains, the clock on the wall ticking loudly over his shoulder. After what seemed like an excruciatingly long time, he finally raised his eyebrows and stared at Boney. "Should I call the police?"

Boney gave a nervous laugh. "It's okay. It's only fake blood. But I need the costume cleaned right away," he said, hoping Mr. Martini would pick up the pace.

Mr. Martini studied Boney's face. "Why? Are you going to a convention or something?"

"It's really important."

Mr. Martini slowly craned his neck, gazing at the clock on the wall as he performed some mental calculations. "It's going to take at least an hour to get these stains out."

Boney frowned. Mr. Martini considered him thoughtfully.

"Do your parents know you're out this late?"

Boney tried to sound as adult as he could. "Yes, of course. I'll be back in an hour, then." He grabbed the pillowcase and Blaster gun and strode toward the door. As he reached for the handle, Mr. Martini called after him.

"You forgot your ticket stub. You can't pick up your dry cleaning without a ticket stub."

"Oh, yeah, thanks."

Mr. Martini fumbled with a giant roll of tickets, the roll uncoiling impudently each time he tried to tighten it. He struggled to tear a ticket from the roll. When at last he did, he slowly ripped the ticket in half and gave one side to Boney, but not before studying the number closely through the magnifying glass.

"And just to let you know," he said, "it's seven dollars to clean soiled Elvis costumes after 10:30 p.m."

Boney nodded, took the ticket, and slipped through the door. Seven dollars?! he thought angrily. What a rip-off. But he had no choice. If he wanted to save Itchy from the circus he would have to shell out. And now he had an hour to kill. He thought about going to the diner next door for a cup of hot chocolate, but that would cost even more money, so he decided to ride his Schwinn around instead. He checked his watch: 10:45. That gave him just enough time to get the suit cleaned and return it before Itchy's dad got home from his show.

Boney placed the blaster gun in the pillowcase and rolled it into a ball, stuffing it between the sissy bars on his bike. He mounted the bike and rode aimlessly through the streets for the longest time, not sure where to go. He looked in store windows and watched a cat hunting a mouse in front of the pet shop. He rode back and forth through the streetlights. He biked in circles in the Top Drawer Insurance parking lot. When he checked his watch again it was only 11:25. If he kept riding straight, he could ride all the way to the train tracks. To the right, he could loop around through town and back toward home. To the left lay the river and the haunted mill. Boney turned left.

After several minutes, he found himself rolling down the street toward the river. He cycled slowly, and the haunted mill eventually came into view. The moon was bigger now, throwing more light on the old ruins.

Boney dismounted, leaning his bike against some tangled bushes. He stepped cautiously to the edge of the stones and stood, peering into the walls. The crickets chirped loudly. Several bats fluttered from the trees overhead, diving in and out of the moonlight after moths. The night breeze tickled the hairs on Boney's arms, raising goosebumps on his skin. He thought about the ghost, the way it had risen, shimmering, from behind the pile of stones across the mill. Boney's breathing grew shallow and light. He looked over at his bike, glistening against the dark bushes. A chill ran up his spine. Maybe it wasn't such a good idea to be here all alone so late. He swallowed hard.

"Is anybody there?" he called.

There was a rustling sound, and then silence.

"Is anybody there?" Boney called out again.

A low moan rose over the stones, and then an eerie voice growled. "Get out! Get out of my mill!"

Boney streaked to the bushes and jumped on his bike, pedalling like a madman up and over the hill until he skidded to a halt outside the cleaners. He dropped his bike to the ground, grabbed the pillowcase, and burst breathlessly through the door.

Mr. Martini stared indifferently back, his hands folded on top of the counter. "What's the matter? Seen a ghost?"

Boney shot a look over his shoulder to make sure he hadn't in fact been followed. Then he glanced at the clock on the wall: 11:46! Less than fifteen minutes to return the suit before Itchy's father got home.

"I'm in a big hurry, Mr. Martini," he said.

Mr. Martini stared at him expectantly.

Boney stared back.

"I can't give you the item without a ticket stub," Mr. Martini said.

Boney fished the ticket from his pants pocket, his hands still shaking as he handed it over the counter. Mr. Martini stared at the ticket through the magnifying glass.

"Late for your big Vegas tour?" he said as he shuffled over to the clothes rack and pressed a large black button on the wall. There was a loud clunk from somewhere in the back of the store. The dry-cleaned clothes lurched forward and began crawling slowly along the rack.

Boney drummed his fingers impatiently on the counter as the second hand of the clock seemed to whiz around.

The clothes continued to crawl. Mr. Martini cocked his head thoughtfully.

"A lot of people love Elvis, but I'm more of a Johnny Cash man myself. Less glitter and fanfare."

At last the Elvis costume appeared. Mr. Martini pressed the black button again, stopping the racks with another loud bang from the back of the shop. He slowly pulled the costume from the rod and hung it up on a hook behind the counter, carefully checking the ticket stub to be sure it matched the ticket on the costume. When he was sure everything was in order, Mr. Martini lifted the costume from the hook and handed it carefully to Boney, who immediately stuffed it into the pillowcase, coat hanger and all.

"That'll be eight dollars," Mr. Martini said.

"But you said seven before!" Boney protested.

"Those blood stains were difficult to remove. I had to use extra-strength chemicals. They're more expensive."

Boney scowled as he crashed the entire contents of his pockets onto the counter, dimes and nickels rolling every which way. It was a good thing he hadn't purchased hot chocolate, he thought, as he quickly counted out the correct change and handed it to Mr. Martini.

Mr. Martini took the change and slowly counted it again, while Boney drummed his fingers more loudly than before. When at last Mr. Martini reached eight dollars, Boney snatched the rest of his coins from the counter and bolted out the door with the costume.

Jumping on his bike, Boney zipped away, pedalling as quickly as he had when escaping the ghost at the mill. By 11:58, he was ditching his bike in the bushes beside Squeak's house and throwing rocks up at Itchy's window, whispering hoarsely for him to come down and get the suit. When the door whooshed open, a horribly deranged Itchy stood on the stoop. His skin was blotchier than usual and his hair looked like a bush fire. He had a knapsack on his back, stuffed with clothes, as though he was preparing to run away.

"It's about time," he moaned.

"I'm sorry," Boney said. "I ran into some trouble." He produced the costume from the pillowcase.

Itchy grabbed it and bolted up the stairs, just as his dad's blue Mercury Cougar pulled into the driveway.

Boney leapt over the rails of the porch so as not to be seen, and ran smack into Snuff coming around the corner from the other side. He pulled the Triple-X Turbo Blaster from the pillowcase and pointed it at the dog, cocking the lever.

"Stay back . . ."

Snuff growled, inching slowly backwards. Boney held him at bay with the gun, long enough to mount his bike and streak down the sidewalk. He skidded up to the garage in a shower of stones, jumped from the bike, and pushed through the door. Racing to the back of the garage, he parked his Schwinn, engaging the kickstand with a sharp kick of his sneaker.

He peeked out the door, Blaster at the ready in case Snuff decided to make an appearance. When he was sure the coast was clear, Boney stepped from the garage and silently closed the door. As he approached the house, he could see from the living-room window that his uncle had gone up to bed at last. Creeping along the walk to the kitchen door at the side of the house, he turned the handle, only to discover it locked.

"Darn," he cursed, sneaking to the front of the house. That door was locked too. Boney sighed. He had no choice but to scale the rose trellis.

"Better just get it over with." He resigned himself, pushing the Blaster into the waistband of his jeans before pulling himself up.

But climbing down had been much easier than climbing up turned out to be. Boney grunted with the effort as he fought through the thorns and branches of the rose bushes. He'd nearly made it to the top, sneakers squashed between the wooden diamonds of the trellis, hands fumbling over razor-sharp thorns, when he heard a loud crack. And then another. And another and another until all at once the trellis tore away from the wall in a thunder of hollow applause. Boney shouted as he and the trellis and his aunt's precious rose bushes came crashing to the ground in a horrible heap, tearing his sneakers from his feet, the Blaster emptying the rest of its water down Boney's pant leg. Lying on the ground in a tangle of rose bushes and splintered trellis, Boney looked up to see

Squeak's horrified face staring down at him from his bedroom window.

In a moment, Squeak was standing over him in his blue flannel space pyjamas, pulling Boney free of the wreckage.

"I told you the whole thing was prickly."

"Uuuuggghhhh," Boney moaned, yanking the Blaster from his waistband.

"Why didn't you just ask me to unlock the door?" Squeak asked.

Boney rubbed his head. His face and hands looked as though he had lost a fight with a dozen angry alley cats. "What are you talking about?"

Squeak held up a large paper clip. "I can unlock any door. I've been practising."

"How would I have known that?" Boney answered indignantly.

Squeak pointed at Boney's sock feet. "Where are your sneakers?"

"In that heap somewhere." Boney waved the Blaster at the mound of rose bushes. "I'll get them in the morning when I clean up this mess."

"What's that on your pants?" Squeak timidly asked.

Boney looked at the giant stain the Blaster had left on his jeans. "It's *water*, Squeak! Geez! Can we get on with it?"

Squeak nodded as he and Boney walked to the kitchen door. Squeak expertly unfolded the paper clip into a straight piece of wire and began jimmying the lock. Within seconds, the mechanism clicked and the door swung easily open.

Boney shook his head incredulously. "Thanks," he whispered, slinking into the house. "I'll talk to you upstairs."

Boney snuck through the darkened kitchen to the hall, then up the wooden stairs to his room, careful to avoid steps three, seven, and nine—the ones with the loudest creaks. In his bedroom, he changed into his pyjamas and placed the Blaster beside his bed. He made a mental note to carry the water gun with him at all times—fully loaded—then uncovered the Tele-tube.

"Mission accomplished," he sighed with relief.

"What about the rose trellis?" Squeak's voice filtered back.

"I'll get up early tomorrow and fix it."

"And the Elvis costume?"

"Delivered under the wire."

"Amazing," Squeak marvelled. "I have to confess, I had my doubts as to whether you would make it. Still, your aunt is going to be furious when she sees her roses."

"Yeah, I know. But there are more pressing issues. I saw the ghost again."

"What?"

"I went to the haunted mill while I was waiting for the cleaners—you know, Mr. Martini can barely see through those glasses. The ghost spoke to me."

"What? What did it say?"

"Boney? Is that you?" his uncle softly called, opening the bedroom door.

Boney threw the towel over the Tele-tube and leaned on the windowsill, trying to look casual.

"Get to bed. I don't want your aunt finding you up."

"Yes, sir."

His uncle waited until Boney climbed into bed. He watched as Boney turned off his bedside lamp and stood in the doorway for several minutes until he was satisfied his nephew would stay put. "Now, no more nonsense. We've had enough excitement for one day."

When his uncle finally left, Boney exhaled.

"That was close."

CHAPTER ELEVEN

FOUR THOUSAND SEQUINS

The next morning, Boney was jolted awake by the sound of his aunt's shrill cries out in the yard. He checked his alarm clock. He'd slept in! Throwing the covers to one side of the bed, Boney raced from his room, stumbling down the stairs to the kitchen. When he opened the door, he saw his aunt and uncle standing before the violated trellis, his uncle's expression more confused than the mangled roses, his aunt's pulled like saltwater taffy into the very picture of tragedy.

"Why, why, why?" she moaned, her eyes searching the heavens, her hands wringing.

His uncle held up Boney's sneakers in his hands. There was no way Boney could talk his way out of this one.

"I'm sorry. It was an accident."

His aunt stood, dabbing her eyes with her red gingham tea towel in the most mournful way.

"Oh my, my, my," was all his uncle could say.

"I'll fix it," Boney promised. "Your roses will be fine.
You'll see." He reached down to lift the trellis but the
wood snapped in his hands, splintering on top of the
mangled roses.

His aunt burst into tears all over again. She staggered to the house, her face buried in her apron.

"Oh my," his uncle said again. He looked at Boney with
a mixture of grief and befuddlement. "Oh my, my, my."

SQUEAK WAS WAITING on the stairs when Boney shuffled
up the walk for school. He didn't even bother ducking
when the paperboy tossed the morning paper his way.

"I heard the whole thing," Squeak confessed.

"I'm so stupid," Boney said, slumping down on the
stairs next to his friend.

"It was an accident. You didn't know the trellis was
structurally compromised. You were just trying to help
a friend."

Boney sighed glumly. "I don't think my aunt will
ever speak to me again."

"I'll help you fix the trellis," Squeak offered. "My

dad has lots of tools, and leather gloves — they should protect our hands from the thorns."

"Thanks."

"Everything will be okay," Squeak consoled him. "You got the Elvis costume back, just like you said you would, and there's still the Invention Convention."

Squeak placed his skinny arm around Boney's shoulders. The two friends sat thoughtfully for a moment. Then Squeak turned his goggled face to Boney.

"Can you imagine Itchy working as a clown in the circus?"

Boney thought about this for a minute, then slowly nodded his head. "Yes . . . I think I can."

The two boys burst into laughter.

"He wouldn't even need a wig," Squeak said.

"Or a nose," Boney added. "Or the big clown shoes!"

Squeak stood up. "Come on. We'll be late for school. And you know Itchy's late enough as it is."

The boys shuffled along the sidewalk, dodging to one side as Mr. Peterson zipped by on his bike, bell jingling merrily as he passed. They clumped up the stairs to Itchy's house, but before they could knock, the door swung violently open to reveal a terrified Itchy and an angry Elvis standing on the threshold. Itchy's red hair looked as though he'd been up all night, running it through a blender.

"Uhhh . . . what's up?" Boney asked.

Itchy's father assumed one of his famous poses, hip stuck out, arm stretched in the air, one finger poised. "Notice anything . . . peculiar? Anything . . . out of the ordinary?" He tossed his greasy hair and struck another pose.

Boney squinted at the white outfit, the same white outfit that had been covered in fake blood only hours ago. There *was* something peculiar about it. It was sparkling clean, that was for sure. Sparkling white, not a trace of the blood from the night before, not a single, itty bitty speck to remind them of their failed attempt at tarring and feathering the mail thief . . . not a single, little . . .

"Sequins!" Itchy's dad cued him at last.

The boys stared at each other in horror. As if the rose trellis debacle wasn't enough!

"I don't know what you boys did, or why," Itchy's dad continued, in a trembling, heartbroken Elvis voice, "but it's gonna take a hunk o' hunk o' love for me to get over this." He gritted his teeth then pouted, holding his hand up in true Elvis style. "Four thousand sequins. The pain. The love."

"We'll fix it, Mr. Schutz," Boney pleaded with Itchy's dad.

"Four thousand sequins," Itchy's dad repeated as he made his exit from the hall.

Boney stared at Itchy's tragic face. "It must have been the chemicals in the dry-cleaning process," he explained. "Mr. Martini said he had to use extra-strength stuff to get all the blood and grass stains out of the suit. And he's blind as a bat. He can barely see. He probably just kept using stronger and stronger chemicals and didn't even notice the sequins were melting off the suit."

"It doesn't matter," Itchy finally rasped, shaking his head. "My dad will never let me live this down."

"We'll fix it right away. I'll get out of school — I'll ask my aunt and uncle."

Itchy just stood there, muttering and shaking his head. "Four thousand sequins . . ."

CHAPTER TWELVE

THE GHOST

Later that morning, Boney stood atop a rickety step-ladder, trying desperately to affix his aunt's broken rose trellis to the wall of the house.

"Look on the bright side," he mumbled, his mouth spiked with nails as he teetered on the stepladder. "At least we got out of school."

Squeak nodded in agreement from his lawn chair, where he was helping Itchy replace the sequins on the Elvis outfit. "My dad didn't even ask for an explanation." He positioned a sequin carefully on the sleeve, holding it in place with his thumb as he pierced it through the middle with the needle to affix it. "You can almost smell where the sequins should go if you look closely enough." Squeak held his goggled face inches from the fabric, secured the sequin, then raised his head thoughtfully. "I still think we should get a mascot."

Boney's hammer tapped an erratic rhythm against the trellis. "What do we need a mascot for?"

"They're good luck," Squeak said.

"Aaaaaaaahhhhhh!" Boney shouted, the nails shooting from his lips and plinking down the ladder to the ground. "These rose thorns are murder!"

"I told you to wear gloves," Squeak sighed.

Boney gripped his hand in pain. "I can't work with your dad's gloves on. They're too big."

Itchy just shook his head. He was sitting in a lawn chair next to Squeak's, his own eyes trained on the pant cuff of his dad's outfit, clumsy fingers fumbling with the sequins and needle and thread. He didn't bother to look up any more when Boney screamed, it happened so often. "Four thousand sequins," was all he said.

Boney retrieved the nails and started hammering at the trellis again. "We need to think about our invention. That's more important than a mascot right now."

"What happened with the ghost?" Squeak asked.

"Ghost?" Itchy gasped, finally looking up from his work. He had sequins stuck all over his hands and face like sparkly fish scales.

Boney shot Squeak a cautionary scowl over his shoulder.

"You know," Squeak blindly continued. "You said it

spoke to you. You never told me what happened."

"What are you talking about?" Itchy demanded, pushing his sewing to one side, sending sequins fluttering brightly to the ground.

Boney stared at Itchy. He wasn't going to mention the ghost at all, given the situation. "It's nothing," he said, turning his attention back to the trellis.

"WHAT ABOUT THE GHOST?" Itchy shouted, jumping to his feet.

"Okay!" Boney shouted back. "Just remember, you wanted to know!"

"I don't believe you," Itchy launched in before Boney had a chance to explain. "We're up to our necks in it," he waved wildly at the trellis and at Squeak, sewing sequins, "and you're still running around looking for ghosts!"

"I was killing time while your dad's suit was at the cleaners," Boney said, defending himself.

"Oh, right!" Itchy snapped. "So, somehow this is *my* fault?"

"I didn't say that!"

"He didn't say that," Squeak corroborated softly.

Itchy held his hands in the air. "I don't want to hear about it," he fumed.

"But you just said you did," Boney replied.

"Oh, yeah, isn't that just like you to twist my words

around," Itchy accused him, clawing at his hair. He stormed back to where his sewing lay draped over the back of the lawn chair. He counted the sequins on the pant cuff furiously. "Fifteen!" he raged. "What's four thousand minus fifteen?"

Squeak opened his mouth to answer but Itchy cut him short.

"It's a lot—I can tell you that! We're going to be sewing until we're forty just to fix this mess."

"Actually," Squeak piped up, "if we keep going at this pace, it shouldn't take us more than a few weeks."

Itchy collapsed in his chair, pulling the leg of the costume into his lap. "What did the ghost say?" he whimpered.

"Do you want to hear about it or not?" Boney asked.

"Go ahead," Itchy conceded. "You're just going to tell us anyway."

"Fine." Boney sat on the top rung of the ladder. "When I was down at the mill the first time, I saw the glasses."

"Glasses . . . ?" Itchy repeated in confusion.

"You know . . . *the* glasses. I told you about them before."

"The wire rims from the story," Squeak added.

"So what, you found some stupid old glasses," Itchy scoffed.

"They were by the firepit," Boney continued, ignoring

Itchy's anger. "When I went to take a look at them, the wall started moaning."

"So . . ." Itchy groused.

"So, it was the ghost," Boney asserted. "It flew out from behind the wall and chased me. And then last night, while I was waiting for the cleaners, I went again, and this time it talked to me."

"What a load," Itchy said, but his eyes were wide with fear.

"It's not a load!" Boney insisted.

"What did it say, then?"

Boney mimicked the sound of the ghost as best he could. "GET OUT! Get out of my mill!"

Itchy snorted. "Obviously, it knows you."

"It's all very exciting," Squeak said. "I can't wait to test the Apparator at the Old Mill . . . once we actually build it."

"Well, you can count me out," Itchy retorted.

"You don't have to come. Squeak and I will test it out."

"Fine."

"I'm hoping the rare earth magnets will arrive in the mail today," Squeak said.

"Good," Boney said. "We can start building the Apparator as soon as they arrive."

Itchy shook his head angrily. "What about my dad's costume?"

"We'll work on that too," Boney assured him.

Itchy grumbled into the cuff of the suit.

"Hey, look! I have one whole row done!" Squeak announced, holding up the sleeve of the costume.

"Great," Itchy scoffed. "Only 3,952 more sequins to go . . ."

CHAPTER THIRTEEN

A Bad Idea

That evening after supper, the Odds gathered around the table in the clubhouse. Itchy's old tire now hung by a rope from the east branch. Boney had placed it there as an apology to Itchy for the way things had turned out with his father's costume.

The rose trellis was fixed as best as it could be, patched with old pieces of wood found in Boney's garage. The sequins would take much longer. Itchy sewed ceaselessly, muttering inaudibly, working by flashlight when the sun started to set.

Boney lit a candle and placed it to one side of the table. Squeak produced the schematics for the ghost detector, unrolling the paper and holding it flat with small pebbles from his pocket.

"Gentlemen . . . may I present the Apparator."

"We've already seen it," Itchy said.

Squeak ignored him, picking up a box from the floor

and opening the lid. "Shall we check the inventory?" He handed Boney a small piece of paper with a hand-written list. Boney began to read as Squeak pulled the equipment from the box.

"Capacitor."

"Check."

"Twelve-gauge copper wire."

"Check."

"Toggle switch."

"Check."

"Bakelite handle."

Squeak produced a black plastic handle from the box. "Check!"

"Weller forty-watt iron."

"Check."

"Ion detector."

"Check."

"Deans ultra-connectors and rare earth magnets."

"Check and check!"

Squeak arranged the items neatly on the table. "This is going to be the best invention ever." He rubbed his hands together, then began assembling the Apparator — soldering connections, coiling copper wire, fitting pieces together.

The boys assembled and sewed, undisturbed by bullies or emergencies of any kind. There was a brief moment when they believed they were being assaulted by eggs, but it turned out to be a shower of acorns from the oak tree that supported their clubhouse.

Eventually, Boney's aunt called him in for bed. The work had to stop for the night, but Boney complied without protest, being extra specially good so as to win his aunt's favour. He had even asked for a second helping of soup casserole at dinner that night, telling his aunt it was the best casserole he'd ever eaten.

THE NEXT MORNING when Boney climbed up the ladder to the clubhouse, Itchy was already there, sewing sequins. He wore a knit vest, striped in wild greens and oranges and browns. One armhole was wider than the other, and the vest looked too large.

"My mom's taken up knitting," he explained when he saw the look on Boney's face.

Boney pulled the Blaster from his waistband and placed it on the table next to the box that housed the half-finished Apparator. He picked up a leg of the Elvis costume and began sewing sequins. He sewed a few to the cuff then cleared his throat. "I was thinking . . . we should have stuck to our original plan."

Itchy stopped, needle poised in the air. "What plan?"

"The plan to lure Larry Harry and Jones and Jones to the Old Mill."

Itchy lowered his sewing in his lap. "We're not doing anything of the kind."

"We still need to get back at them."

Itchy held up a sleeve. "Haven't we made enough mistakes already?"

"But our original plan was foolproof. Nothing can go wrong. We don't have to borrow anybody's costume or anything. We just lure Larry and Jones and Jones to the mill and let the ghost do the work."

Itchy rolled his eyes. "And how are we supposed to lure those creeps to the mill?"

Boney opened his mouth to answer, but he was interrupted by a sudden clattering from Escape Hatch #1.

"Hold still," Squeak could be heard saying before his head appeared at the top of the ladder, red face sweating behind his gigantic goggles. "I figured out our mascot problem," he proudly announced.

"What mascot problem?" Boney asked.

"Ta-da!" Squeak said, producing Snuff through the hole in the clubhouse floor.

"Squeak, no!" Boney shouted as Snuff exploded from Squeak's hands, snapping and snarling like the devil unleashed. The dog lunged across the clubhouse and leapt on Boney's leg, grabbing the cuff of his pants and pulling Boney to the floor with a horrible thump. Boney reached for the Blaster, but his arm hit the supply shelf on the wall, tearing it down and sending empty cracker boxes and peanut butter and jelly jars flying across the clubhouse. Itchy sprang on his dog in a flurry of sequins, only to send the cutlery drawer springing from its spot on the table, the box with the Apparator sliding dangerously close to the edge, knives and forks and spoons crashing in a silver heap to the floor. Snuff yelped as several spoons hit his back, and he began snarling and snapping with even greater fury, convinced Boney had thrown the cutlery.

"Snuff, no!" Squeak yelled as Boney kicked and cursed, until all at once he grabbed the Blaster and fired, sending the surprised dog skittering with a yelp down Escape Hatch #3.

"Snuff!" Itchy cried, looking down the hole where the dog had disappeared. But there was only a puff of dirt in the air where Snuff had hit the ground.

"There he goes!" Squeak said, pointing down the street to where Snuff was running furiously toward home.

The boys gazed around the clubhouse. It looked as though a small tornado had touched down.

"Perhaps Snuff isn't the best mascot for us after all," Squeak conceded.

Boney looked at his torn pants in disgust. "He put

a hole in my cuff. You know he hates me, Squeak. Why would you even try to bring him up here?"

"I was hoping he could get to know you and you could be friends."

Boney gestured with the Blaster. "We'll never be friends."

"Not if you keep shooting at him," Squeak sniffed.

"He really isn't good for much," Itchy admitted.

Boney pulled himself up from the floor, securing the Blaster in his waistband. "Just forget about the whole mascot thing, Squeak. Look at this mess!"

The boys began cleaning the clubhouse, reaffixing the supply shelf to the wall with twice as many nails as before, organizing the cutlery drawer to its former condition, and checking the Apparator to make sure it hadn't been damaged. They even found a piece of plastic and covered the reference library bookshelf, just in case. When they were done, Boney and Itchy collapsed on the clubhouse floor. Squeak continued to work on the Apparator.

"I can't take it any more," Itchy sighed. "First Larry Harry wrecks our lives, then my dad's costume gets ruined, and now Snuff trashes our clubhouse."

"I told you, we're going to get Prisoner 95 once and for all," Boney insisted.

"I don't want to hear about it," Itchy said. "Running after ghosts in spooky old haunted mills is crazy. We'll just end up hurting ourselves, or getting beat up even worse than we already do."

"We *will* need to go to the Old Mill," Squeak said, grinning broadly, "because the Apparator is finished." He tightened a screw on the handle, then held it up for the others to see. "Gentlemen, may I present the $500 prize-winning entry at this year's Invention Convention."

The Apparator glistened in the light, its black handle shining, its clear tube wrapped artfully in copper wire. On the handle was a small red switch and hand-painted letters that read "*The Apparator.*"

"It looks great," Boney said. "We can test it tonight."

"I thought you were grounded for life," Itchy said.

"I'll ask for three helpings at dinner tonight, if I have to. My aunt will let me do anything after that."

Itchy folded his arms across his chest. "I don't care. I'm not going to the mill."

"Fine," Boney said. "Stay here by yourself. But don't cry to us when the mail thief comes looking for you."

Itchy's mouth flapped up and down in futile protest. "This is so unfair."

CHAPTER FOURTEEN

THE BIG TEST

That night, the Odds rode in a tight group toward the mill: Boney on his metallic-blue Schwinn, Squeak swerving with his goggle vision on his red Raleigh cruiser, and Itchy on his mom's old green CCM, complete with flowered grocery basket strapped to the handlebars. They wove through the darkened streets, punching in and out of the lamplight until the lights disappeared and the street turned to gravel. When they reached the top of the hill leading to the Old Mill the boys skidded to a stop, the dust kicking up in little clouds around their bikes.

"Now remember," Boney said, "we keep our bikes close, just in case anything goes wrong."

Squeak nodded. Itchy gulped.

Boney pushed off with his foot, coasting his Schwinn slowly toward the stone ruins. Squeak and Itchy fol-

lowed close behind, Itchy's front tire rubbing dangerously against Squeak's rear tire.

"You're going to make me crash," Squeak hissed
over his shoulder.

"Sorry," Itchy apologized, applying the brakes.

As they reached the abandoned mill, Boney dismounted and guided his bike carefully through the
opening in the stone foundation. Squeak did the same.
Itchy stood at the entrance peering cautiously into the
ruins.

"Come on," Boney rasped.

Itchy followed reluctantly, yanking his mom's bike
across the rocks. The bike clattered over the stones, elic-
iting dirty looks from Boney and Squeak.

"Sorry," Itchy apologized again.

The boys leaned their bikes against the stone wall.
Itchy moved to engage his kickstand, but Boney stopped
him.

"You might not want to do that."

"Why not?"

"We might need to make a quick getaway."

The boys peered nervously through the dark night
air. Boney stepped forward, his sneakers grinding
loudly over the gravel. Itchy and Squeak watched from
the safety of the stone wall.

"Is there a reason why we have to test the Apparator in the dark?" Itchy asked. "Don't ghosts come out during the day, too?"

"All reported sightings of the ghost have been at night," Squeak informed him. "It only makes sense that we come in the dark if we hope to get an accurate reading."

"That's what I was afraid of," Itchy grumbled, pulling a Big Turk bar from his back pocket and ripping open the wrapper.

"How can you eat at a time like this?" Squeak asked.

Boney grimaced. "How can you eat that at all? Big Turks don't even qualify as chocolate."

Itchy took a large bite from the bar. "It helps me relax."

Boney walked across the ruins to the firepit. "Hey, guys, over here. This is where I was standing when I saw the ghost. The glasses should be here somewhere." He searched the ground, kicking through the dirt with his sneakers. "They were here before, I swear."

"Don't touch anything," Squeak advised as he pulled the ghost detector from his messenger bag. "We don't want to disrupt the ectoplasmic energy."

"Definitely not," Itchy said, opening another chocolate bar and taking a bite. He looked warily around the ruins, chewing quickly.

Squeak held the detector in the air. "I feel we should say a few words before we run the test. You know, kind of like what the Queen does at a ship christening ceremony."

"Fine," Boney agreed.

Squeak cleared his throat. He assumed an official air, speaking in a lower voice, the kind an important scientist might have. "After many days of effort, we are finally standing here, three scientists, dedicated to unearthing the truth behind nature's mysteries, dedicated to a study of the intricate fabric of this world's subtle complexities, dedicated to —"

"Can we get on with it?" Itchy snapped through chocolate-covered teeth.

Squeak turned indignantly toward Itchy. "Some of us take this sort of thing rather seriously."

"Well, I take my life seriously," Itchy retorted.

Squeak rolled his eyes and turned to Boney. "Sir, if you're ready . . ."

When Boney nodded, Squeak pressed the red switch on the handle of the Apparator with his thumb. There was a click, and a low hum began to emanate from the detector. The tube at the end of the black handle began to pulse green, the light reflecting in the thick lenses of Squeak's goggles like two luminescent squid.

"How do we know when it's detected a ghost?" Boney asked.

"The light changes according to the ectoplasmic energy field," Squeak explained, mesmerized by the humming device. "It evolves from green, which means safe, to yellow, which means caution, to red, which means a ghost is in the area."

"It's turning yellow now!" Itchy said, pointing to the glowing tube.

"Cool," Boney said, watching as the pulsing light grew in intensity.

"It's turning red!" Itchy wailed. "Let's get out of here!"

"Not yet," Squeak said. "We need proof that we're actually detecting a ghost."

"Like what? A dead body?"

"It could just be fluctuations in the barometric pressure causing an increase in static electricity affecting positive air ion levels," Squeak explained. "We need to know for certain that the detector isn't giving a false reading."

"Yes, of course," Itchy agreed, sarcastically. "We wouldn't want a false reading."

The Apparator continued to change. A low moaning rose up from behind the stone walls.

"Ha ha, very funny," Itchy said to Boney.

"It wasn't me," Boney said.

Itchy looked at Squeak.

"It wasn't me either," Squeak said.

The detector began to buzz. The tube turned fire-engine red as the moaning grew louder, filling the air.

"It's the ghost!" Itchy screamed, pointing across the mill to a shimmering form rising from behind a pile of rubble.

"Run for it!" Boney yelled.

Itchy grabbed Squeak's shirt and sent him tripping to the dirt. The ghost detector fell out of his hands and rolled wildly across the ground. Boney stumbled over Squeak's sprawled legs and went flying to the ground as well.

"STAY OUT OF MY MILL!" the ghostly voice growled.

The shimmering form streaked toward the Odds as they scrambled over each other to reach their bikes. The abandoned Apparator glowed angrily on the ground.

"We're getting out!" Itchy shouted, grabbing his bike and jumping on the seat. His feet pounded against the pedals and dirt sprayed everywhere as he launched toward the opening in the wall, only to hit a rock and catapult head first over the handlebars into the grass.

Boney and Squeak ditched their bikes. They grabbed Itchy's arms and attempted to heave him to his feet, but his legs turned instantly to overcooked spaghetti noodles.

"STAY OUT OF MY MILL!" the ghost shrieked, rushing across the ruins, its dark mouth gaping, its empty eye sockets trained on the boys.

"AAAAAAAAAAHHHHHH! It's curtains for us!" Itchy screamed as the ghost fell upon the Odds in a heap.

Determined not to go down without a fight, Boney kicked and shouted, grabbing the ghost by the head and pounding furiously with his fists. Squeak lay like a paralyzed hamster on the ground, eyes and mouth frozen open.

"Ow!" The ghost yelled as Boney continued to kick and punch.

"It *is* curtains," Squeak suddenly announced, emerging from his paralysis.

"Huh?" Boney said, still struggling with the ghost.

"It's curtains," Squeak exclaimed, grabbing one end of the shimmering ghost and yanking with all his might. "Real curtains. It isn't a ghost at all," he said as he uncovered a dusty little man cowering beneath the fabric.

"Oh, blast," the little man exclaimed.

Boney jumped angrily to his feet. "What do you think you're doing, running around, scaring the heck out of people?"

The man lowered his eyes sheepishly. "I live here,"

he said, in a voice that made him sound as if he gargled with gravel. He adjusted his wire-rimmed glasses on his nose.

"Hey! Those are the glasses I saw by the firepit!" Boney said.

"I put them there," the man said. "I wanted to take advantage of the legend."

"The legend of the missing boys?" Squeak asked as he retrieved the Apparator. He checked it over, switching it on and off several times.

The man nodded.

"So why are you going around impersonating a ghost?" Boney demanded.

The man shrugged. "It's the only way I can keep people out of the mill."

"Despicable," Itchy said, examining the remnants of the squashed chocolate bar in his hand.

"Odd," Squeak added.

The man eyed Itchy's chocolate bar hungrily.

Itchy gobbled the last of the bar. "We should beat him up," he said, his mouth full of chocolate. He pointed to the curtains. "Look, he just painted that stupid face on himself. Pathetic."

The man cringed. "Please, I didn't mean to hurt you. I only wanted to keep you away."

"Why?" Boney asked.

"It's—it's the only home I have," the man stammered, clinging to the fabric curtain.

The boys exchanged puzzled looks.

"My name is Rufus," he said, holding out his hand. He wore an old pair of navy-blue mechanics' coveralls, the legs rolled several times at the ankles and wrists. There was a worn oval patch sewn to the coveralls with the name "Charlie" stitched in red letters.

"How come your badge says 'Charlie' if your name is Rufus?" Itchy asked suspiciously.

The man looked at the patch on his chest. "Oh that." He lowered his hand. "Someone . . . uh . . . left these here years back."

"And where'd you get those glasses?" Itchy asked.

Rufus smiled. "I found them. Don't know if they're helping or not."

Boney shook his head. "So you pretend to be a ghost to keep kids away."

"Not just kids," Rufus said. "Anybody. I heard about the ghost after those kids went missing all those years ago."

"In 1952," Squeak said.

Rufus nodded. "Yes, that's right. It was 1952. Nasty business, that."

"How do we know you aren't the guy responsible for those kids going missing?" Itchy asked.

"Me?" the man said incredulously. "Why, I wouldn't hurt a fly."

"How do we know that?" Itchy said. "How can we trust the word of a guy who runs around in a curtain moaning like a ghost, wearing somebody else's clothes?"

"I have nowhere else to go," Rufus said apologetically. "Besides," he added, almost proudly, "I help keep vandals away. They were destroying what was left of the property."

"And you've never seen any ghosts around here?" Boney asked.

"None but me," the man answered.

Squeak sighed loudly. "Well . . . there goes the official test of the ghost detector."

"I'm sorry, boys," Rufus said. "I didn't mean to spoil it for you." He eyed the detector in Squeak's hand. "Do you mind if I take a look?"

Squeak shrugged and handed him the device.

Rufus turned the Apparator over in his hands, admiring the coiled wire and red switch. "Mighty fine piece of work. It uses an air ion detector in conjunction with a variable tube radio capacitor fitted with a dielectric insulator."

Squeak's eyes widened behind his goggles. "Yeah! How did you know?"

"I used to be quite handy myself, designing and building things." Rufus flipped the switch on the detector. It crackled and hummed wildly in his hand. He flipped the switch again, and the light in the tube slowly ebbed to a cold grey. "You just may have yourself something here."

Itchy snatched the detector from the man. "Yeah, sure. If we were looking for weird old men running around in curtains impersonating ghosts, we'd win the Invention Convention for sure."

Rufus lowered his eyes dejectedly. "I'm really very sorry."

"Don't worry about it," Boney said. "It was exciting for a moment to think the detector actually worked." He turned toward his friends. "Come on, guys. Let's go."

"We won't be bugging you again, mister," Squeak said glumly as he took the Apparator from Itchy and stuffed it in his bag. He swung his bag over his shoulder and grabbed his bike, rolling it through the opening to the path.

The man waved as the boys cycled away. "It was nice meeting you all. Come back and visit sometime."

CHAPTER FIFTEEN

LEFTOVERS

Back at the clubhouse that night, Itchy and Boney continued to sew sequins on the Elvis costume while Squeak tinkered with the Apparator.

"We can't enter the convention with a faulty device," Squeak said wistfully. "I just don't understand why it didn't work. I've checked all the connections, re-soldered all the points, and tightened the screws. Even if the Apparator was picking up errant static electricity, it shouldn't have responded so violently." He turned the detector over in his hands, the same way Rufus had. "Maybe I need to reduce the gauge of the copper wire ... or try replacing the insulators in the capacitor ..."

Itchy looked up from his sewing. "Maybe it's so sensitive it can pick up *fake* ghosts as well."

Squeak frowned, peering along the length of the tube.

Itchy reached over and plucked a peanut butter and

honey cracker from the tall stack on the table next to him. "Do you think that old guy was telling the truth?"

"About what?" Boney asked.

"You know . . . about being homeless and protecting the mill and all that."

Boney shrugged. "I don't know. Guess there's no way to find out for sure."

"He had us pretty scared, though, didn't he?" Itchy said.

"Yeah," Boney laughed.

"We should have known it wasn't a real ghost anyway," Itchy continued.

"Why?"

"He was too short."

"Right." Boney shook his head. "I guess ghosts can be short, too, Itchy."

"Yeah, I guess," Itchy agreed.

"If they're short in real life, they should be short in the afterlife, right?" Boney reasoned. "He seemed interested in the Apparator, though. I wonder if he could help us make it work."

"Incoming!" Squeak suddenly shouted, grabbing the Apparator and diving to the clubhouse floor.

Itchy wadded up the Elvis costume and dove on top of it, protecting it from the exploding eggs. Boney ducked beneath the window as an egg whizzed past his head and splattered on the wall behind him. Larry's horrible, hoarse laugh filled the air. The boys looked at each other in shock.

"That was close," Boney said. "Is everyone all right?"

"Aye, aye," Squeak said.

"Ditto," Itchy groaned from his place on the floor.

Boney slowly raised himself up so he could see out the window. "Coast is clear."

Squeak continued to lie on the clubhouse floor, staring at the ceiling thoughtfully. "I wonder what da Vinci would have done in a situation like this."

"Being bombed by eggs?" Itchy asked.

Squeak gave him a puzzled look as he rose to his feet, placing the Apparator carefully on the table. "Perhaps I made a mistake in the calculation for the coil frequency . . ."

"It's a good thing we covered the reference library," Boney said. He took a rag, dipped it in the pail of water, and began wiping egg off the plastic.

Itchy stowed the Elvis costume safely on a shelf before dunking the mop in the bucket and sloshing water on the clubhouse floor. "Lousy egg-bombing convicts," he cursed.

"What were you saying about Rufus before we were so rudely interrupted?" Squeak asked Boney.

"I was wondering if he could help us out," Boney

said. "He seemed to know a lot about electronics and that kind of stuff."

Itchy eyed him warily, stuffing peanut butter and honey crackers in his mouth as he scrubbed the floor. "What do you mean?"

"He said he used to build stuff. It wouldn't hurt to ask him to take a look at the Apparator."

"He already looked at it," Itchy said.

Squeak stared forlornly at his invention. "Maybe he was just being polite. I think we should ask him. My dad's too busy to help us, and I could sure use a second opinion."

Itchy rolled his eyes. "How do we know we can even trust the guy? I mean, he might be a total psycho for all we know. He lives in an abandoned mill, running around with a curtain over his head."

"Come on, Itchy, he's just an innocent guy who doesn't have a home. We don't have to marry him. We just need his advice."

"How do we know he'll even agree to help us?" Itchy asked.

"Simple," Boney said. "We'll make him an offer he can't refuse."

"We'll threaten to call the cops and turn him in for murder?"

"No. We'll bring him food. You saw the way he looked at your chocolate bar."

Itchy quickly stuffed the last of his crackers into his mouth. "I'm not wivving him anyfing," he protested, cracker crumbs spraying everywhere.

"You don't have to," Boney said. "I'll give him something, for heaven's sake."

Itchy nodded with finality, swallowing with a huge gulp. He pointed at his throat. "Milk," he croaked.

Squeak tossed him a small carton of milk from the cooler. Itchy wrenched it open and drained the carton in one big swig.

"You're going to give yourself indigestion if you keep that up," Squeak admonished him. "Anyway, I think Boney's idea is worth a try."

Itchy rubbed his stomach happily. "Ahhh . . . that's better."

"William!" Boney's aunt called from the kitchen door. "Bedtime!"

Boney groaned but answered politely, "Yes, Auntie!" He threw the rag into the pail. "Tomorrow, after dinner, we rendezvous at the clubhouse, then visit Rufus. Agreed?"

"Agreed," Squeak said.

Itchy pouted, folding his arms across his chest. "Oh, fine. Agreed."

CHAPTER SIXTEEN

Henrietta

The next day at school, the Odds managed to avoid Larry Harry and Jones and Jones for several classes. They slipped from homeroom undetected, and made it through geography and English without so much as a small incident. But by science class, Larry was wadding up paper and spitting it through a straw into Itchy's hair, which was so wild and unkempt that he couldn't even feel the impact. The Odds simply focused on their science lab, where a Bunsen burner flamed beneath a test tube of unidentified purple liquid, until a particularly large spitball hit the test tube, knocking it to the desk and setting their entire station on fire.

The Odds leapt off their stools, shouting unintelligibly. Mr. Harvey sprang from behind his desk, grabbed the fire extinguisher, and blasted the fire with foam until it was out. The lab station resembled a giant burnt marshmallow. The teacher even blasted several shots at

Itchy's hair, convinced it was part of the problem.

"What happened here?" Mr. Harvey demanded.

Boney lifted his scorched lab manual from the desk. It was dripping with foam from the extinguisher. "It was an accident, sir," he said, scowling at Larry Harry, who by this time was innocently working away on his side of the room. Jones and Jones snickered as Itchy drew some foam from his hair and discovered the spitballs.

"Disgusting! I can't go through the rest of the day like this."

But as bad as the situation was, he had to admit that spitballs in his hair was better than getting creamed in lacrosse, which is exactly what happened next, when Boney and Itchy went out for gym.

Out at centre field, Boney stared back at Larry, lacrosse stick in hand, body poised to spring. He shot a look over at Itchy, who gripped his lacrosse stick in goal, his entire body shaking with fear. Larry bared his teeth like a wolverine. Colonel R. blew the whistle. Boney dove, snatching up the ball, only to have Larry trip him with his stick. Boney thumped to the ground, the ball bouncing across the grass. Larry scooped it up and drove it at Itchy, who was hit by Jones and Jones as he rushed forward, crashing him backwards into the net.

"It's a plot," Itchy groaned as he and Boney limped

home after school that day, Squeak at their side. "They're determined to kill anyone with an IQ over fifty."

Boney gritted his teeth in pain. "Don't worry. Larry's going to be sorry he was ever born."

Itchy stared at him incredulously. "*I'm* sorry I was ever born. It's going to take me months to get these spitballs out of my hair."

Boney and Squeak helped him up the stairs to his house.

"See you after dinner at the clubhouse tonight," Boney said. "And don't forget to bring something to eat, if you can."

"Eat . . . right," Itchy said as he staggered into his house and shut the door.

"See you soon," Squeak called out to Boney as the two boys parted ways.

When Boney entered the kitchen, the smell of frying onions made him forget his agony. Was it possible his aunt was actually cooking something good?

"Smells great," he said, just as his aunt dumped a can of soup into the pan.

Boney grimaced and made his way to his room, dropping his books on his bed. He did some science homework, starting a new notebook to replace the one ruined in class that day. He thought about his essay for English for a while. When he grew bored of that, he washed carefully behind his ears to be presentable at dinner. He didn't want his aunt to have any reason to keep him detained that night. Boney pored over his math text then, finishing the last of the equations assigned that day in class. At 6:30 on the dot, his aunt called him down for dinner.

At the supper table, his uncle was in his usual spot, reading the paper. He smiled as Boney took his seat, then frowned when he saw the grey glop on his plate. Folding his paper, he sighed resolutely and began to eat. Boney did the same, eating methodically until his plate was clean.

"May I have another serving?" he asked, holding up his plate.

"Well, of course, dear," Boney's aunt gushed, heaping another glop onto Boney's plate.

His uncle watched with concern as Boney finished his second helping, then pushed his dishes to the centre of the table.

"May I be excused?"

"Have you finished your homework, young man?" Boney's aunt asked as she cleared the dishes.

"Yes, ma'am," Boney said, leaving the table and pulling a plastic container from the cupboard.

His aunt eyed the container suspiciously. "Just where do you think you're going with my best Tupperware?"

Boney put on his most sincere face. "I wanted to share some of your delicious casserole with my friends."

His uncle whistled softly under his breath.

His aunt twisted her mouth to one side. "Don't they have food of their own?"

"They do," Boney conceded, "but their parents don't cook as well as you." He forced his mouth into a smile.

His aunt beamed proudly. "You can use the old margarine tubs," she said, handing Boney several plastic containers from under the sink.

"Thanks."

Boney began ladling out the casserole, the grey glop thumping into the containers. He flattened it down with a wooden spoon, secured the lids, then placed the tubs in a paper grocery bag. He added several slices of bread for good measure, then scoured the cupboards for something sweet. He found a tin of bran muffins and decided they were better than nothing, even if they were hard as hockey pucks. He wished he could bring something good, like chocolate chip cookies or brownies, but his aunt didn't believe in feeding children "such junk."

"Sorry, Rufus," Boney apologized as he tossed a few hard muffins in with the bread and casserole.

Folding the paper bag, Boney carried the care package to the clubhouse.

Itchy was already waiting, wearing an ill-fitting

black-and-yellow knit toque and swinging languidly in the old tire, his mom's bike leaning against the oak tree. "There's one for each of us," he said, producing an identical yellow-and-black toque from his coat pocket.

Up in the clubhouse, Boney pulled the toque over his head and rolled the rim until he could see properly. The two boys unfolded the Elvis costume and began to sew while they waited for Squeak.

Eventually, they heard a struggling sound, and soon Squeak's head appeared in Escape Hatch #1. He stared at Boney and Itchy's hats.

"There's one for each of us," Boney said, pointing to a third toque on the table.

"Oh . . . are we establishing a dress code?"

Boney turned to Itchy.

"My mom thought it'd be nice to have matching hats, seeing as we have the clubhouse and all."

"That was nice of her," Squeak said. "I bet you can't guess what I've got."

"Leftovers?" Boney said.

"Wrong!" Squeak raised his hands, grinning from ear to ear. "It's another mascot!"

"Squeak, no!" Boney yelled as Itchy lunged to cover the Elvis costume.

Squeak opened his hands. But instead of a dog, he unleashed a small, fuzzy chick onto the clubhouse floor.

"A bird?" Itchy asked.

"A hen," Squeak answered proudly. "My dad ordered her for me from the farm co-op. I figured she would make a great mascot because when she's old enough to lay eggs we'll have a continuous supply of ammo to use against Prisoner 95 and his fellow convicts."

The little chick peeped as it began scratching and searching the clubhouse for bugs.

"See how good she is?" Squeak beamed. "She can reduce the standing bug population and she doesn't mind being high up in a tree."

Itchy handed Squeak the toque from the table. "I hate to burst your bubble, Squeak, but chickens can't fly."

"I am aware of that," Squeak answered, obediently donning the toque. "They *roost*. They fly just enough to get up and down safely."

"If you roll up the rim, it'll fit better," Boney said. He looked at the chick. "I think she's cute. What's her name?"

Squeak worked the rim on the toque. "I think we should call her Henrietta."

The chick peeped as though in agreement.

"Henrietta it is," Boney said. "What does she eat?"

"She likes everything," Squeak said, adjusting his hat. "But I bought her some feed, just in case." He pulled a handful of ground corn from his pocket and scattered it over the clubhouse floor. The chick began greedily pecking and scratching at the corn.

"I have a box for her, too," Squeak said. He climbed back down the ladder and then reappeared with a box and an old towel. "She can sleep in here at night." He placed the box on the floor, pulled one side down to create an entranceway, and carefully arranged the towel inside. The little chick hopped into the box and nestled in the towel.

Itchy leaned over to take a closer look. "I guess having a chicken for a mascot isn't so bad. In fact, it's kind of appropriate." He scratched the chick on the top of her head. "Better start laying eggs fast," he said, then returned to his sewing. He affixed another sequin to the costume and held it up proudly. "Can you believe it? It's finally done!"

"We have to celebrate!" Boney said, opening the cooler and producing three cans of ginger ale. He tossed one to each of the boys then cracked his open with a loud hiss. "To a job well done!"

The boys clinked their cans together.

Itchy guzzled his soda, slurping loudly. "I never thought it was possible." He let out a huge burp.

Boney and Squeak did the same.

"Now we can focus on our invention," Squeak said.

Boney turned to Squeak. "Hey, what'd you bring for Rufus?"

"A TV dinner."

"How's he supposed to heat it?" Itchy asked.

Squeak shrugged.

"What'd you bring?" Boney asked Itchy.

Itchy produced half a dozen purple Pixy Stix. Boney raised his eyebrows.

"What?" Itchy said defensively. "I wasn't about to give him my Pez."

"Even Squeak's uncooked TV dinner is better than that," Boney admonished.

"Actually, TV dinners are precooked," Squeak corrected him. "They just need to be heated up."

"Right . . ." Itchy said. "What'd you bring, then, Boney?"

"*Supper Surprise Casserole.*"

"Are you trying to kill him?"

"It's the only thing I had. I brought bread, too, and muffins."

"Mmmmmm . . . delicious," Itchy mocked.

"It's better than a bunch of stupid Pixy Stix — and all the same flavour, too."

"Shall we go, gentlemen?" Squeak said, interrupting the argument.

Itchy folded his father's costume carefully, placing it in a bag to protect it on the short trip home. "Take care of the clubhouse while we're gone!" he called out happily to Henrietta as he climbed down the ladder.

Henrietta peeped cheerfully from her box.

THE THREE FRIENDS pedalled quickly down the street, skidding to a stop in front of Itchy's house. They marched in procession up the stairs and through the door, up to the second floor and down the hall to the closet, where Itchy hung the costume with great reverence.

"Never again," he vowed as he straightened the bag covering the suit.

"Never again," Squeak echoed.

Snuff appeared from Itchy's bedroom. Boney lifted the hem of his shirt, revealing the Blaster. The dog cowered, slinking silently back into the shadows.

"Come on, guys," Boney said. "Let's go."

Back on the street, the Odds pedalled to the Old Mill. When they reached the dilapidated stone foundation, they rested their bikes against the wall and carried their food offerings to the firepit.

"Where are the rest of the Pixy Stix?" Boney asked

Itchy, who had produced only two sticks instead of six.

"I got hungry on the way," Itchy said, his tongue a brilliant purple.

"You're hopeless," Boney sighed. He placed his care package on the log by the pit. Squeak and Itchy did the same.

"Rufus," Boney called out in a loud whisper. "We've brought something for you."

"Some crappy casserole and a frozen TV dinner," Itchy called out before Boney could smack him on the arm.

"Who's there?" a voice rasped from behind a pile of stones.

"It's us," Boney said. "The kids you scared the other night."

"That could be anyone," Squeak whispered to Boney.

"The three kids who discovered your identity," Boney corrected himself.

The boys waited expectantly. At last Rufus appeared from behind the rocks. Boney held up the care package.

"What've you got there?" Rufus asked.

"Food," Boney said.

Rufus eyed the bags hungrily. He rubbed his hands together in anticipation.

"It isn't the greatest food in the world," Boney apologized.

"Oh, it's fine," Rufus said, pulling the casserole and the frozen TV dinner from the bag.

Itchy reluctantly handed over the last two purple Pixy Stix. "Here," he said. "We brought you these, too."

Rufus's eyes lit up when he saw the candy. "Much obliged," he said, with genuine gratitude.

The three boys watched as Rufus tucked into the food like a hungry dog. He ate silently, burning through the casserole and bread. It wasn't until he was halfway through the TV dinner that he slowed down enough to actually speak. He looked up from the tray. "Nice hats," he said, sopping up gravy with a bran muffin.

Boney took the opportunity to ask his question. "Mr. Rufus . . ." he began.

"Just Rufus, son. No need for formalities here."

"Rufus . . ." Boney corrected himself. "We were wondering if you could maybe help us out with something."

"What is it?"

Squeak produced the Apparator from his bag.

"Ahhh . . . yes." Rufus pushed the food to one side and took the device, turning it over in his hands. "This is a mighty fine piece of work, boys. Couldn't have done any better myself."

"Except it doesn't work," Squeak said.

"Well, now, let's see . . ." Rufus accepted a screw-driver from Squeak and began making adjustments. He tightened the coils and peered along the length of the handle. He held the tube to his ear and tapped it lightly with one finger. He checked the wires leading to the switch and clicked it on and off several times, then listened to the tube again. "Seems fine to me," he said, handing the device and screwdriver back to Squeak.

Squeak flipped the switch. The Apparator began to glow green, then quickly pulsed from yellow to burning-hot red. He snapped the switch off in disgust. "I just can't figure it out. Maybe it's picking up frequencies from the hydro lines." He craned his neck around to look.

Itchy sat down next to Rufus and began eating the rest of the cold TV dinner. "It's not so bad," he said, ges-turing with a chunk of half-frozen Salisbury steak.

Rufus laughed. "You boys remind me of my own sons. They were good boys, just like you. They used to work around here. We all did. I keep hoping I'll see them some day."

"Did they invent things too?" Squeak asked, sitting cross-legged in front of Rufus.

Rufus nodded. "Oh, yes, lots of things. Egg-timers, small water wheels, steam-whistle calliopes, and a merry-go-round that ran on a tractor engine. They even invented a saw that could cut a log in quarters in less than ten minutes."

Boney frowned but said nothing. A saw that cut logs in ten minutes was hardly even practical. "Where are your sons now?" he asked, sitting next to Squeak.

Rufus lowered his eyes. "They're gone . . . long gone. I keep waiting for them to come back, but they never do."

There was an uncomfortable silence as the boys searched for something to say.

"We were really hoping to win the Invention Convention," Itchy finally said. He gave a big sigh, chewing thoughtfully on the TV dinner bun. "First prize is five hundred dollars."

"We really want to beat Larry Harry," Squeak added.

"Who's that?" Rufus asked.

"Prisoner 95, until recently known as the Fart King," Itchy said between bites. "He's evil and mean and he's a big, stinking, egg-bombing cheater."

"He sabotages our convention entry every year," Squeak said. "That's how he wins."

"He's our mortal enemy," Boney added.

Rufus looked at the boys with concern. "I'm really sorry to hear that, boys. Life is hard enough without that kind of suffering. I wish there was something I could do."

Boney rose to his feet. "Well, we appreciate your help all the same."

"Come back anytime, boys," Rufus said, patting his stomach. "Anytime." He opened one of Itchy's Pixy Stix, tipped the stick back, and showered the purple powder over his tongue. "Cheers!" he said.

CHAPTER SEVENTEEN

THE INVENTION CONVENTION

Weeks went by. The Odds dodged Larry Harry as best they could, on and off the playing field. When they weren't in school, they were holed up in their clubhouse, playing with Henrietta, doing their homework, or fussing with the Apparator. But despite their best efforts, the Apparator wasn't ready when the time came for the Invention Convention.

The boys wandered glumly through the school gymnasium over their lunch hour, Squeak bumping listlessly into the corners of tables, Itchy swimming in an oversized orange hand-knit sweater, as they looked at the convention entries. Students bustled about, securing bristol board displays and organizing their tables. They were the lucky ones who actually had entries to show. They even got to take the morning off school to set up.

The Odds stopped in front of Edward Wormer's display.

"A potato clock?" Itchy snorted, flapping an orange sleeve at the invention. "You've got to be kidding me. That's not an original invention."

Wormer rushed out from behind the display. He snapped a pen from the holder in his dress shirt and clicked it. "Could you move along, please? I'll be happy to sign autographs after I win."

"Dream on," Itchy said. "That's not even your idea. I ought to eat that potato."

Wormer stretched his skinny arms protectively in front of his display. Boney tugged Itchy along.

"There are some really good entries this year," Squeak sighed. "I spent so much time on the Apparator, I didn't even consider the possibility of entering something else. There are only three days left before the judging begins. I can't possibly think of something groundbreaking in three days."

The Odds reached Stacy Karns's display. She and her girlfriends stood chattering behind their table, dressed in identical pink outfits, their hair clipped back with identical clasps. They didn't even acknowledge the Odds.

"Cheating Chopsticks?" Itchy said, picking up a pair of chopsticks glued to a clothespin. He read the title on the display. *"For people who can't master the art of eating with sticks.* How stupid!"

Squeak took the chopsticks, testing their action. "It's actually quite brilliant. Sometimes the simplest inventions are the best."

"They're certainly more marketable," Boney said.

Squeak sighed again. "Perhaps I was aiming too high with the Apparator."

The Odds moved along to Simon Biddle's entry.

"Dog Collar with a Light," Boney said, reading the display board. "Now that is actually a really good idea."

Squeak nodded dejectedly. "Yes, it is."

Simon Biddle smiled proudly from behind his table, his metal braces flashing.

"Where's Larry's entry?" Itchy asked.

Squeak pointed voicelessly across the gymnasium. The Odds drifted over to Larry's display.

"The Cushy Cover?" Itchy said in disbelief.

Boney shook his head. "It's a toilet seat made of sponge."

Itchy gave the seat a poke. "I guess he needs all the help he can get."

Larry popped up menacingly from behind his display. "Keep your hands off the merchandise, loser!"

Itchy recoiled in horror. Boney clenched his jaw.

"We'll see who the loser is after the convention."

"Oh yeah?" Larry sneered. "Where's your entry, Bonehead?" He gazed arrogantly around the gym.

"It's coming," Boney snapped back. "And it's a lot better than a stupid sponge toilet seat."

"We'll see about that. I've won every convention for the last three years."

"That's because you cheat," Squeak piped up.

Larry made a fist in his face. "How'd you like me to knock your goggled lights out?"

Boney grabbed Squeak and Itchy, dragging them away from Larry's table and out the gymnasium door. "Come on, guys. It won't help if we get ourselves beat up."

"Yeah, run away, you sissies," Larry called after them. "You can come visit me in the winner's circle next week."

Itchy folded his arms over his chest. "If he wins the convention with that stupid invention, I'm going to do something drastic."

"Like what?" Boney said. "Skip breakfast?"

Itchy frowned. "I don't know. I just wish we could stop him once and for all."

Squeak shook his head. "Even a sponge toilet seat is better than nothing at all." He pulled the defunct Apparator from his bag. "I still don't understand why it won't work."

Boney's face suddenly brightened. "Itchy, you're a genius!"

Itchy looked cagily around. "What're you talking about?"

Boney grabbed the Apparator excitedly. "We may not be able to win the convention, but we can still get back at Larry."

Squeak and Itchy stared in confusion. "How?"

"We can use the Apparator! We'll let him know we're testing our invention at the Old Mill. When he shows up to sabotage our apparatus, we unleash the ghost."

"Great plan," Itchy quipped. "Except *there is no ghost!*"

"Wrong," Boney said. "There's Rufus."

Squeak blinked. "Rufus?"

"Yes, Rufus. Don't you get it? We arrange with Rufus to do exactly what he did to us. That way the Apparator isn't a total failure."

Itchy scrubbed at his hair. "I don't know, Boney . . . maybe we should just cut our losses and think about an invention for next year."

"We could bring the Polaroid camera," Squeak offered. "That way we could document the carnage and post the photos the next day at school."

Boney snapped his fingers. "Now you're talking!"

"What if Rufus doesn't want to do it?" Itchy asked.

"Simple. We'll bring more food."

Squeak adjusted his goggles. "Let's do it."

"Great," Boney said. "Let's meet in front of Itchy's after dinner. Everyone, bring food — that means you too, Itchy."

CHAPTER EIGHTEEN

GETTING THE GHOST

"Where are you going with all this food?" Boney's aunt demanded.

"We get hungry when we play in our clubhouse," Boney fibbed.

His aunt sighed. "Well, I can't say I blame your friends for wanting to eat my home cooking. I'm sure their parents don't give a second thought to good nutrition, with so much junk food in the world. And poor Squeak must be half starved, what with his mother gallivanting around the country." She whipped her tea towel from her arm and snapped it viciously in the air at some invisible buggy intruder.

Boney smiled and nodded, dropping a margarine container of casserole like a brick to the bottom of a paper bag. He tossed in a few hard muffins and a container of jiggling lime-green gelatin studded with candied fruit.

Stuffing the bag in his knapsack, he proceeded to the garage and hopped on his Schwinn.

Squeak was already waiting in front of Itchy's on his bicycle when Boney arrived. Itchy appeared at the door, wearing a long, multicoloured, hand-knit scarf and munching on a turkey drumstick.

"Where's your food for Rufus?" Boney asked.

"It's right here," he said, holding up a small brown paper bag.

Boney frowned. "What's in it?"

"Bread and butter," Itchy happily declared.

"No turkey?"

Itchy chewed on the drumstick. "This is the last of it."

Boney scoffed. "Right. Let's go."

The Odds rolled along the road to the mill, Itchy munching on the drumstick as they went, Squeak swerving back and forth with his goggled vision. When they reached the ruins, the boys parked their bikes and stepped gingerly into the open space.

"It's so spooky at night," Itchy said, tossing the turkey bone to one side and licking his fingers.

"It's hardly after dusk," Squeak said.

Itchy pointed to the sky. "Look at the moon. It's coming up already, and it's nearly full. Wasn't the ghost supposed to come out when the moon is full?"

Squeak nodded. "That's what the reported sightings all say."

The Odds stood in the centre of the ruins. Boney called out quietly, "Rufus . . . are you there?"

There was a scrabbling sound from across the mill.

"Is that you, Rufus?"

"Who's there?" a voice called out.

"It's me, Boney. And Itchy and Squeak."

Rufus appeared timidly from behind a pile of stones.

"We brought you more food," Boney said, holding up the brown bag.

"Well, isn't that nice," Rufus said, taking the bag and opening it greedily.

Itchy produced his bag, too. "I brought bread and butter."

"And another TV dinner," Squeak offered. "It's actually hot this time."

Rufus sat down happily on the log by the firepit and began hungrily tucking in. "Isn't this just the nicest surprise. You boys are so kind."

The Odds watched as Rufus tore through the casserole and muffins, then peeled back the cover on the TV dinner. He dipped Itchy's bread and butter heartily into the gravy, the way he'd done before, savouring the taste as though it were a five-star meal. When he was finishing off the peas, Boney approached him with their request.

"Rufus . . . we were wondering if you could help us with something."

Rufus lapped up the last of the TV dinner. "Sure, boys. What is it?"

Boney looked at Itchy and Squeak, who looked back skeptically.

"We have this problem . . . remember the bully we told you about, the guy we call Prisoner 95?"

Rufus thought for a minute then nodded. "Yes, I do remember you mentioning him."

"Well . . . we thought if maybe we scare him and his friends, they might leave us alone."

"Scare them?" Rufus said. "What do you have in mind?"

Rufus continued to eat while Boney laid out his plan.

When Boney finished talking, Rufus placed the empty containers back in the bag, wiped his face and hands clean with a handkerchief that he produced from his breast pocket, and eyed the boys with a look of concern. "I don't know, boys . . ."

"You just *have* to help us, Rufus," Boney pleaded. "Just this once. If you scare Larry Harry, we promise not to ask you for anything else again."

Rufus tucked his handkerchief back in his pocket and sighed. "It isn't easy for me, you see. I'm really quite shy. And I'm afraid . . . of what might happen. I just want a normal life. These things can get out of hand.

Someone could get hurt." He squinted up at the moon.

"It's just this once," Boney said. "It would mean so much to us."

Rufus stared at his shoes for a moment. "When do you want this to happen?"

"Tomorrow night," Boney said. "There are only three days left before the convention is judged, and we'd really like Larry Harry to get what's coming to him before he sabotages someone else's invention."

The three boys held their breath as they looked hopefully at Rufus. Rufus sat back on the log, thinking. He rubbed his chin and shook his head.

"You boys have been very kind to me," he said at last. "And you really do remind me of my own sons. I wish there was something I could have done to help them along in life." He paused thoughtfully. "Besides, I think it's time for me to leave this place."

"So you'll do it?" Boney asked.

"Yes. I'll do it. Just this once."

"That's so great, Mr. Rufus," Boney gushed. "You won't regret it. I promise."

BACK AT THE CLUBHOUSE, the boys analyzed every detail of their plan to get even with Larry Harry.

"But how are we going to get him to come to the Old Mill?" Itchy asked from his position on the floor, chin on his folded hands, as he watched Henrietta scratching at her supper. He took a small pinch of the hen's grain and put it in his mouth, nodding with approval.

"Simple," Boney replied. "We'll send him a note and tell him to meet us there. He can't refuse an opportunity to beat us up."

"What if the plan doesn't work?" Itchy said. "What if it backfires, like every other plan we've hatched over the years?"

"Don't be silly," Boney said. "The plan is good and it *will* work. I promise."

"If it doesn't, we'll have to go back to Plan H," Squeak said, pulling more corn from his pocket and scattering it on the clubhouse floor.

"What's Plan H?" Itchy asked.

"Henrietta," Squeak said. "She should be laying eggs by the spring, and then Larry Harry will be sorry he ever messed with us."

"Oh, he'll be sorry all right," Boney said.

Itchy rolled onto his back. "There's still one more week of lacrosse. I hope Larry doesn't kill us before we have the chance to get back at him."

"Roger that," Boney said.

CHAPTER NINETEEN

A Meatloaf
Monkey Wrench

The next morning, the Odds were on their best behaviour. Even Miss Sours, who was on a yardstick rampage in homeroom, could find no fault with them. The boys breezed through their classes, determined to make it through the day without incident so as not to disrupt their plan to get even with Larry Harry that night.

"We just have to make it through gym," Itchy prayed as he held his lacrosse stick in goal.

Boney stared back at Larry Harry, who growled like a rabid dog from centre field. Boney squinted his eyes, bolstered by the knowledge that by nightfall he would have the last laugh—at Larry's expense.

Colonel R.'s whistle pierced the air. Boney dodged as Larry ploughed past him, snapping up the ball. He turned, driving the ball at Itchy, who raised his stick instinctively and, causing great surprise to everyone, caught the ball with a grunt as it whizzed toward his head. Jones and Jones charged toward Itchy, who gaped at the ball in momentary disbelief then quickly flipped it as if it were a ticking bomb to Boney, who was back on his feet and holding his stick expectantly in the air. Boney caught the ball and drove it down the field to Wormer, who ducked, allowing the ball to zip over his head and into Larry's stick. Larry drove the ball to Jones, who flipped it to Jones, who drove it at the net, hitting Itchy square between the shoulders as he turned to avoid the ball, knocking him breathless to the ground.

Colonel R.'s whistle trilled, indicating end of play and game over. Boney rushed over to Itchy, who lay sprawled over the grass, his skinny arms and legs splayed out like a lanky white starfish.

"Itchy, that was fantastic!"

"I think my back's broken."

"Take him to the nurse," Colonel R. barked as Boney and Itchy limped off the field.

"Did you put the note in his locker?" Itchy asked, his eyes glazed with pain.

"Yeah," Boney said. "Just before we came down for gym. Now all we have to do is get to the Old Mill and wait for nightfall."

The nurse patched Itchy together with a bandage

around his back and another around his head. When she was finished, the two boys went looking for Squeak and found him hiding behind the stacks in the library. As they left the school, Itchy pulled his yellow-and-black toque over the bandage on his head.

"It's a good thing my mom made this hat so big."

"How do we know Larry will show up at the Old Mill?" Squeak asked again.

"We don't know," Boney said. "But I'd bet my stash of jawbreakers that he will. He can't refuse my offer."

"What did you write in the note?" Squeak asked.

"I told him to meet us at the Old Mill after dark . . . or else."

"Or else what?" Itchy piped up, a look of panic on his face.

"Or else . . . nothing. I didn't say what."

"So . . . just a general 'or else' threat," Squeak qualified.

"Yeah, something like that," Boney said.

Itchy suddenly turned as though to run away. Boney and Squeak grabbed his arms. Itchy's knees buckled. "I don't like the sound of this, Boney. Larry has it in for me already. Look at me! I'm covered in bandages from head to toe. If this thing fails tonight, you may as well plan my funeral!"

Squeak helped steady Itchy on his feet, then pulled the Apparator from his messenger bag. "I just can't help feeling disappointed," he said, glumly. "I had such high hopes for this invention."

Just as he said this, the Apparator was wrenched from his hand. Itchy shouted with terror at the sight of Larry Harry.

"What's this, pipsqueak?" Larry said, brandishing the Apparator.

Boney lunged for the detector. "Give it back."

Larry tossed the Apparator from hand to hand. "Is this your big secret invention? A nightlight?"

"It's an apparitions detector," Squeak said, trying to grab the Apparator.

"Speak English, dog-breath, or I'll stuff you in a sewer hole."

Squeak took a guarded step back. "It's a ghost detector."

"Aaaahhhh! Don't tell him," Itchy howled.

Larry grabbed Squeak by the shirt. "A ghost detector . . . how does it work?"

Squeak gaped at Larry from behind his goggles as Itchy frantically flagged a passing car for help. When the car actually slowed down, Larry lit out with the Apparator in hand.

"I'll see you tonight, suckers!" he shouted, crumpling up Boney's note and tossing it in Itchy's face.

"He took the Apparator!" Squeak cried.

"What are we going to do?" Itchy wailed.

"We don't need the Apparator for tonight," Boney said.

"We're doomed," Itchy moaned.

"No we're not," Boney assured him. "Come on."

The three boys walked down the street, Itchy looking cagily over his shoulder, Squeak dragging his heels. The sound of Elvis music could be heard as they approached Itchy's house. When they walked up the stairs, the front door flew open to reveal Mr. Schutz striking a pose in the doorway in his newly sequined outfit. He glanced at Itchy's bandages and curled his lip. "You betta watch yourself, boy. You're turning into a mummy . . . or something."

Itchy's mom rushed to the door wearing something that looked like a cross between a hand-knit sweater and a full-length wool gown. "Oh, my poor baby!" She began kissing Itchy all over his bandaged head.

"I'm okay, Mom," Itchy said.

"How did this happen?" she demanded.

"I'm fine, Mom," Itchy insisted. "It was just a stupid lacrosse accident."

"I'm going to call your teacher."

"Oh, no. Please, Mom. That would only make matters worse."

"Don't worry, Mrs. Schutz," Boney said. "After tonight, this will never happen again."

"What's happening tonight?" she asked.

Squeak elbowed Boney hard in the ribs.

"Oh, uh, we're going to practise some moves to help Itchy improve his game. We'll pick you up later, okay, Itchy?"

Itchy disappeared into the house with his mom.

"Don't forget your special-effects kit," Boney reminded Squeak as he dropped him off at his house. "And don't worry about the Apparator. I'll think of a way to get it back."

Squeak nodded listlessly and disappeared inside.

When Boney walked into the kitchen of his own house, his aunt was there, balanced on top of a chair in her best apron and snapping her gingham tea towel like a bullwhip at the fridge.

"Oh, William, thank heavens!" she gasped. "There's a spider on the fridge and it just about killed me!"

Boney stared at her in horror. His aunt only wore her best apron when company was coming. And he could smell his most dreaded meal of all cooking in the oven: *meatloaf.*

"Please, William," his aunt cried. "I think it's poisonous."

"Venomous," Boney corrected her as he grabbed a margarine tub off the table and dragged a chair over to the fridge, hoping to capture the spider and let it outside before his aunt lashed it to death. But she was whipping and snapping the towel so wildly that he had to dodge for his life. He could barely see the top of the fridge, let alone a little spider hiding out there. When the towel came dangerously close to his eyes, Boney ducked, only to be clipped in the ear.

"Owwwww!" he howled, and the margarine tub tumbled to the floor.

"There it is!" his aunt shrieked, whipping and snapping faster than ever.

The spider, little more than a black speck, dashed out from behind an amber vase on the fridge and flew through the air, straight at Boney's aunt. She screamed hysterically, falling backwards off her chair onto the margarine tub. The tub burst, splattering margarine all over everything.

"Ahhhhhhhh!" she cried, holding up her hands. "The spider slimed me!"

"It's only margarine," Boney said. "I thought the tub was empty."

Boney's uncle scurried into the kitchen. "Oh, my." He helped his wife from the floor.

"Did you see it?" she asked. "It was the size of my hand."

Boney looked at his uncle and shook his head, indicating the true size of the spider with his thumb and forefinger.

Boney's uncle sighed. "Now, now, dear. You don't want to get yourself worked up before our company arrives."

"Company?" Boney gulped with dismay. "Who?"

"Mr. and Mrs. Sampson," his uncle spluttered.

"Mr. and Mrs. Sampson!" Boney wailed. "They're coming here?"

His uncle nodded.

"But why?! All they do is eat and talk and laugh about nothing. You said you'd never invite them over again after the last time!"

Boney's uncle looked sheepishly over at his wife.

"Mrs. Sampson is a friend of mine from high school," Boney's aunt snapped. "They're very nice people . . . perhaps a little loud and messy . . . but they're coming all the way from Poughkeepsie, and I'm not about to turn them out because you two haven't a clue how to behave in good company."

"Yes, yes," Boney's uncle sighed. "You'd better go upstairs and get changed," he told Boney. "They'll be here any minute."

CHAPTER TWENTY

OPERATION SPEEDO

B oney walked reluctantly from the kitchen, grabbing the olive oil from the table as he went. He would need the oil later on to help with his plan. That is, if his plan was still possible. With company coming, he wouldn't be allowed out. He'd have to stay and be polite and listen to endless conversations about nothing.

In his bedroom, Boney slumped in front of the Tele-tube, ears red from his aunt's wayward tea towel. "Squeak. Are you there? Over."

"Squeak here."

"We've got a situation," Boney said. "A fly in the ointment."

"Worse than Larry Harry stealing our invention?" Squeak's dejected voice floated through the Tele-tube.

"Much worse. It's Mr. and Mrs. Sampson. They're coming for dinner. And there's meatloaf in the oven."

"Ehhhh . . . sorry to hear that." Squeak gulped.

"They stayed until midnight the last time, if I remember correctly. What's the game plan?"

"Operation Speedo."

"You own a Speedo?"

"I have to get sent to bed early so I can sneak out undetected."

"Affirmative," Squeak said. "Predicted success rate?"

"Unknown at this time," Boney answered. "But the situation is dire. I repeat, the situation is dire. Over."

"Roger that."

Mr. and Mrs. Sampson were already seated at the dining-room table by the time Boney appeared wearing nothing but a Speedo, some flippers, and a snorkel mask. The conversation came to an abrupt halt, glasses and hors d'oeuvres suspended in the air and mouths gaping as Boney flipped up to the table and took his seat.

"Hello," he said.

"W-what in the world . . ." his aunt gasped. She turned apologetically to her dinner guests, who stared at Boney as though he had three heads.

"How odd," Mr. Sampson mumbled.

Boney smiled as though everything was normal. "Could you pass the salt?" he asked Mrs. Sampson, who clutched at her blouse.

"The boy must have a fever," his uncle said, placing his hand on Boney's forehead.

Boney yawned heavily. "I'm fine. May I have some delicious meatloaf, Auntie, please?"

Boney's uncle scowled. "Just as I thought. He's running a temperature. You'd best go to bed." He stood up, yanked Boney's chair from the table, and helped him to his flippered feet.

Boney gave another big yawn. "I'm so sleepy. Will you save some delicious meatloaf for me, Auntie?"

"Go," his uncle said, pointing to the stairs.

Boney flip-flopped sideways up the steps, taking the opportunity to catch his breath several times for dramatic effect. When he was safely back in his room, he closed the door and flippered happily to the Tele-tube.

"Mission accomplished," he whispered.

"Most impressive," Squeak said. "I never imagined the Speedo was such a powerful weapon. What's the ETA for the Old Mill?"

"Thirty minutes and counting. I just need to get my stuff together. Relay details to Itchy. Over."

"Roger that."

Boney covered the Tele-tube, then changed from his Speedo into his jeans and dark-blue sweatshirt, pushing the Blaster water gun into his waistband. He would slip out of his room, then sneak down the stairs and out the front door while his aunt and uncle were distracted by their guests. If he was quiet enough and avoided steps three, seven, and nine, he should be able to leave the house undetected.

Taking a pile of dirty clothes from his bedroom floor, Boney arranged them under his covers in a shape that resembled his body. For the head, he stuffed a small pillowcase, placing his yellow-and-black toque on top. Then he positioned the fake head in the bed so that it looked as if he were sleeping with his back to the door. With the lights turned off, the dirty-laundry dummy struck a very convincing figure.

Boney looked out his bedroom window. The sun was already sinking below the houses on Green Bottle Street. Soon it would be dark. If all went well, by this time tomorrow, Larry's bullying would be a thing of the past.

Unscrewing the lid from the bottle of olive oil, Boney poured some on the hinges of his door so they wouldn't creak when he opened it to escape. The oil worked beautifully; the door opened silently.

The stairs were another matter altogether. He knew he should avoid steps three, seven, and nine, but he had forgotten about the loose board on stair thirteen. The board creaked like a coffin lid as Boney placed his weight on the step. From where he was standing, he could see his uncle being bored to death at the table and his aunt pretending to laugh at some stupid joke of Mr. Sampson's.

His aunt turned slightly as the stair groaned beneath Boney's foot. He stopped dead in his tracks, waited until his aunt turned back toward her guests, then navigated the rest of the stairs to the front door.

The olive oil was applied to the hinges of the front door as well. When he was sure he'd used enough to make a difference, Boney placed the bottle of oil on the floor next to the wall and proceeded to open the door — ever so silently, ever so slowly.

Just as Boney was about to slip through the door, there was a terrifying shout and he was sure he'd been caught. But it was just Mr. Sampson telling one of his stupid stories.

Crouching low, Boney snuck past the dining-room window and crept along the walkway to the garage to retrieve his Schwinn. He manoeuvred the bike to the sidewalk and made his way to Squeak's. Once there, Boney threw a pebble at his friend's bedroom window. Squeak appeared in the window for only a moment before disappearing and reappearing at the front door of the house, his military messenger bag stuffed with special-effects paraphernalia.

"How did you get past your aunt?" he asked as he grabbed his own bike and walked with Boney to Itchy's.

"It wasn't too hard," Boney said. "I used olive oil on the door hinges."

"What if they discover you're gone?"

"They won't. I made a dummy out of old clothes so they'll think I'm still there."

Squeak nodded in admiration.

"Did you bring your camera?" Boney asked.

Squeak opened his bag, revealing the Polaroid.

"Good."

When they reached Itchy's, the boys found Snuff waiting on the porch. But instead of attacking Boney the way he usually did, the little dog whined and quickly slunk down the stairs into the shadows.

"What's gotten into him?" Squeak asked.

Boney secured his Blaster in his waistband. "Beats me."

Peering through the living-room window, the boys could see Itchy's father practising his Elvis routine. He gyrated and danced, striking impressive poses and singing into a dish detergent bottle. Itchy's mother sat watching on the couch, a pleasantly tolerant look on her face.

"She's probably seen the same routine a million times," Boney said. "Maybe it's time to start working on some new material . . ."

Just then, Itchy appeared at the door, wearing a hand-knit fuchsia balaclava. "Thank heavens you're here," he said. "I couldn't stand to listen to that song one more time. He's been rehearsing for hours." He looked at Squeak's messenger bag. "I hope you know what you're doing."

"Is that really necessary?" Boney asked, pointing to the balaclava.

"I don't want to be recognized."

"But anyone could tell it's you," Boney said.

Itchy looked to Squeak for support.

Squeak nodded. "It's true."

Itchy pulled the balaclava from his head and stuffed it in the mailbox.

"Come on," Boney said. "We should hurry. We don't want Larry to get to the mill before us."

CHAPTER TWENTY-ONE

THE DEMON OF THE HAUNTED MILL

The three boys jumped on their bikes and pedalled quickly down the street. They crested the hill toward the mill, the full moon rising red and round over the trees.

"It's going to be totally dark soon," Itchy said as they approached the ruins.

Squeak squinted at the sky. "The moon should provide some light. I hope Rufus remembers we're coming."

Itchy looked nervously over his shoulder. "Me too."

When they reached the mill, Boney slowed to a stop and jumped from his bike. Squeak and Itchy did the same. They peered into the ruins. It was deathly quiet.

"Doesn't look like anyone's here," Itchy announced. "I guess we can go home."

He turned to leave but was stopped by Boney.

"Come on, Itchy. We told Rufus we'd be here."

"But *he's* not here," Itchy protested.

"He's probably hiding somewhere," Squeak said.

Boney rolled his bike toward the bushes. "We'd better stash our bikes, just in case."

Itchy shot him a look. "In case what?"

"Well . . . we don't want the prisoner and his convicts sabotaging our bikes or anything."

Itchy pointed to his bike. "This is my mom's bike. If anything happens to it, I'm dead."

Boney waved him off. "Quit worrying. Your mom can just knit you a new one," he joked.

"Ha, ha, very funny."

"Nothing will happen," Boney said. "It's just a precautionary measure."

"Yeah, sure," Itchy groused under his breath as the boys wheeled their bikes into the bushes. He tucked his bike behind a yew bush, then quickly pulled it back out again. He did this several times until Boney stopped him.

"What are you doing?"

"I want to make sure I can get to my bike quickly if I have to."

Boney rolled his eyes. "Come on. Rufus will wonder where we are."

The boys stepped quietly over the rubble into the

mill. They stood on the periphery, staring into the dark space. The moon stared back. Squeak adjusted the Polaroid on the strap around his neck, finger poised for ghostly action.

"Rufus," Boney quietly called. "Are you here?"

The moon disappeared behind some clouds. The boys shifted in their sneakers.

"Rufus," Boney called out again.

"*Rufus . . .*" the mill echoed eerily.

The Odds exchanged nervous looks.

"Rufus," Boney called out again.

Again the name called back to him. And then a rustling sound rose from the wall behind them.

"Rufus . . . is that you?" Boney asked.

"*Rufus, is that you?*" the voice said.

The boys stood, listening. All at once there was a horrible shriek and Larry Harry and his twin sidekicks ran hollering into the Old Mill.

The Odds screamed at the top of their lungs, staggering backward into the ruins.

Larry pointed mockingly. "Hah! Look at the sissies. They were really scared! What's the matter, babies? Thought you saw a ghost?"

"We weren't scared," Boney retorted.

"Yes we were," Itchy said.

"Well, you should be scared," Larry sneered, "'cause

Jones and Jones are gonna make hamburger outta you."

Jones and Jones grinned menacingly, punching their fists into their palms. Boney drew the Blaster from his waistband.

"Stay back or I'll shoot."

Larry drew the Apparator from behind his back, brandishing it wildly.

Squeak gasped. "Don't shoot, Boney!"

Boney dropped the Blaster to the ground.

"I would've smashed it earlier," Larry taunted, "but I wanted you to see me do it."

"Where's Rufus?" Itchy hissed.

Larry flipped the switch on the Apparator. The rod began to hum, the green light pulsing softly. "What a brilliant invention," Larry scoffed. "A stupid green tube."

"It's not stupid," Squeak said.

"Yes it is," Larry snarled.

"No it isn't!" Squeak insisted.

Larry raised the Apparator in the air. "Yes, it is. It doesn't do anything."

Just as he said this, the Apparator began to crackle, and the light pulsed from green to yellow to orange.

"Oh look, boys, now it's orange. Isn't that special," Larry mocked.

"There are still a few bugs to iron out," Squeak said, defending his invention.

Larry laughed derisively. "The only bugs that need ironing out are you three."

He drew back his hand, threatening to smash the Apparator to the ground. But he was stopped mid-swing by a low moan rising from the rubble across the mill.

"What was that?"

The Odds looked at each other.

"Rufus," Boney whispered.

Another moan sounded from the rubble, this time deeper and louder.

"Who's doing that?" Larry demanded.

"Uh ... guys ..." Squeak said, tapping on his friends' arms. "Look at the Apparator."

The Apparator began to whine, and the tube changed colour from orange to a fiery red as sparks sizzled along the copper wire.

Larry held the Apparator out in horror. "What's wrong with this stupid thing?"

All of a sudden, the firepit roared to life. The Odds jumped, staring at the flames in disbelief.

"How'd they d-d-do that?" Jones and Jones stuttered.

"Ha, ha! Very funny, nerds," Larry said. "It's just a stupid science trick. Anyone can do it."

Itchy stared at Boney. "Did you do that?"

Boney shook his head, then looked at Squeak, who shrugged his shoulders in confusion.

"Must be Rufus," Boney said.

Just as he said this, the moans filled the air and the ghost appeared, rising slowly from behind the stones, its diaphanous form shimmering hauntingly in the blood-red moonlight. The Apparator began to shriek like a kettle on the boil, the bulb burning hot as coals.

"A g-ghost!" Jones and Jones shouted.

"Get your camera ready," Boney told Squeak.

"It's not a ghost," Larry said, staring anxiously at the Apparator. "It's just a stupid guy in a sheet." He turned and pointed at the Odds. "You're gonna regret this, nerds! Come on, let's get 'em, guys!"

Jones and Jones stood frozen, pointing at the ghost in terror.

"It's just a stupid guy in a sheet!" Larry insisted.

But Jones and Jones wouldn't budge.

Larry stomped his foot in rage. "I'll prove it to you!" He charged the ghost, grabbing one corner of the sheet and yanking with all his might. "See? I told you it was just a fake!" he shouted.

All at once, there was an ear-splitting boom and a brilliant white light exploded from beneath the sheet like a nuclear bomb. It blasted the boys across the ruins, drowning their screams in a roaring wind. Squeak hurtled to the ground with a horrible thud, his camera snapping wildly. Above the mill the clouds gathered like a whirling flock of ravens, twisting in the sky. Lightning flashed like a giant strobe. And then the demon appeared, as huge as a zeppelin, its face a terrifying skull, its eye sockets raging with fire. It streaked past the moon, skeletal hands outstretched as it torpedoed toward Larry Harry, who screamed hysterically on the ground. The demon swooped over him, flying instead toward Jones and Jones. The twins tried to run but were snatched up by the spectre's claws, carried through the air, and dropped like stones in the river.

The demon turned its fiery eyes upon Larry, who stumbled toward the bushes. The ghoul dove again, screeching through the air as it caught Larry by the back of his shirt and tore up into the clouds. It arced over the trees, hanging against the clouds for just a moment, with Larry kicking and screaming, before it launched the bully into the mill pond. Larry howled as he fell, and he hit the water like a bag of wet cement. Thrashing wildly, he flailed to the edge of the pond and scrabbled up the bank, slipping and sliding in the mud. He ran into the woods, with Jones and Jones running frantically behind him. The demon shrieked in hot pursuit, shooting bolts of lightning at their feet as they ran. And then, just as suddenly as it had appeared, the ghost corkscrewed into the sky like a missile and vaporized in an explosion of light. It took the fire in the pit with it, leaving only a puff of smoke in its place.

"Wow!" Squeak said, his goggles askew on his face. Polaroid pictures littered the ground.

"Rufus," Boney whispered.

"Is it gone?" Itchy moaned, his eyes scrunched shut.

The boys rose cautiously, peering around the mill in shock. Boney searched through the dust to one side of the fire. He bent down and pulled something from the dirt.

"The glasses!" He held them up, moonlight glinting off the lenses. "I wonder who Rufus really was . . ."

"Do you think we'll ever see him again?" Itchy asked.

Boney shook his head. "I don't know. But I do know one thing for sure: we'll never have to worry about Larry Harry again."

"Hey!" Squeak shouted, pointing across the yard. "The Apparator!" He ran to retrieve the device and dusted the dirt from the handle. The tube was dark once again, with wisps of smoke steaming from the coils. Squeak considered his invention thoughtfully. "I guess it worked after all."

"Yeah," Boney said. "You can congratulate yourself on that." He kicked at what was left of the Triple-X Blaster on the ground. It was shattered in a hundred pieces.

"That's why I insisted on using Bakelite for the Apparator handle," Squeak said, knowingly.

Itchy collected the Polaroid snapshots. "Oh, boys . . . we have some amazing stuff here."

The Odds gathered around the photos.

"You can see the ghost perfectly!" Boney said. "And Larry looks scared out of his mind!"

"These will be great for our convention display!" Squeak said.

Itchy stared at the photos, beaming. "We have the best invention ever."

"I thought you didn't want anything to do with ghosts," Squeak said.

"I don't," Itchy replied. "But I really want to win that prize money!"

"He scares me," Larry whimpered again.

Colonel R. looked over to where Boney stood. "Are you kidding me, Harry? Get off this bench and play!"

Larry shook his head. "No. You can't make me."

Colonel R. glared at Jones and Jones, who sat quivering next to Larry. They shook their heads in refusal.

"We're not playing either."

"Has everyone gone soft around here?"

Colonel R. clenched his whistle in his teeth. He snatched Larry's stick from his hand and tossed it to Wormer. "You're up, Filbert!" he shouted.

"It's Wormer, sir."

Colonel R.'s whistle pierced the air. "Play ball!"

BACK IN THE LOCKER ROOM, Itchy happily changed into his jeans. "You know, I think I might actually enjoy lacrosse," he confessed, pulling on a new blue sweater vest.

"It's a great game," Boney agreed. "Now that Larry Harry is out of the picture."

"Did you see his face?" Itchy gloated. "He was scared silly."

"I wonder what got into him," Boney said, laughing.

"We have to find Squeak and tell him. He'll love it."

CHAPTER TWENTY-TWO

THE REAL GHOST OF THE HAUNTED MILL

The next morning at school, Colonel R. blew on his whistle. "Take your positions!" he yelled.

Itchy stood in goal, lacrosse stick held in front of his face. Boney grabbed his stick and jogged to centre field. The boys waited for the game to start, but Larry Harry refused to leave the bench.

"What seems to be the problem, here?" Colonel R. shouted. He marched over to where Larry was sitting and blasted his whistle in his ear. "Come on, Harry, get on the field!"

"I'm not playing against him," Larry said, ducking his head as he gestured toward Boney.

"And why not?" Colonel R. demanded.

Larry lowered his voice to a whisper. "He scares me."

"What?" Colonel R. cupped his hand around his ear.

Just then, the change room door burst open and Squeak rushed in.

"We won!" he squealed, jumping around like a monkey.

Boney grabbed his friend. "Whoa whoa whoa . . . what are you talking about?"

"The Invention Convention!" Squeak shouted. "We won!"

The boys raced from the change room to the gymnasium. Flying through the doors, they could see the giant blue ribbon pinned to the top of their display. They clung to each other, jumping up and down with excitement.

"I knew we'd win!" Boney said. "I just knew it! San Diego, here we come!"

BY 7:00 THAT NIGHT, the gymnasium was crowded with students and their parents, milling around, admiring the Invention Convention displays. Itchy and Boney stood proudly in front of their table, while a journalist from the local newspaper furiously snapped photos.

"Now . . . one with the whole family," the man said, gathering everyone together.

Itchy's father and mother huddled next to Boney's aunt and uncle.

"That's my boy," Itchy's father said. "A chip off the old block."

"We're so proud of you, William," Boney's aunt cooed.

"Very proud," Boney's uncle echoed.

"But where's Squeak?" Boney asked Itchy. "He said he'd meet us here."

"There he is!" Itchy said, pointing across the gym.

Squeak scurried up, a huge book under his arm, his face lit with excitement. "I found him!" he said, heaving the book onto the display table.

"Who?" Boney and Itchy asked.

"I looked everywhere and I thought I'd never find him, but I did, eventually, in the *Encyclopedia of Rural History*."

"There's an *Encyclopedia of Rural History*?" Itchy asked.

Squeak thumped the book open, pushed his goggles to the top of his head, and pointed to a black-and-white photo on the page. "Look! It's him — it's Charlie!"

Boney and Itchy peered at the old photo. Staring back at them was picture of a man, clad in blue coveralls, wearing thin wire-rimmed glasses.

Boney looked at Squeak with surprise. "It's Rufus!"

"Not Rufus," Squeak said. "Charlie. His real name is Charlie — just like it said on his coveralls. His name was

Charlie O'Reilly, and he died in an accident at the mill in 1897. One of the beams gave way and he was trapped without food and water in a room beneath the mill. He died of thirst and hunger, the book says."

"That would explain why he eats so much," Itchy said, pulling a chocolate bar from his pants pocket.

Boney scratched his head. "But why did he tell us his name was Rufus?"

Squeak turned around and pointed to the logo on his messenger bag. "He took the name off my bag."

"I don't get it," Itchy mumbled, his mouth full of chocolate.

"It's quite simple. He saw the name Rufus on my bag and he borrowed it to disguise his identity."

"What for?" Itchy asked.

"If we'd known his real identity, we'd have never talked to him in the first place, would we?" Squeak explained.

Itchy mulled this over. "I guess not."

"Of course we wouldn't have," Boney jumped in.

"There's more," Squeak said, quickly flipping the page of the book. "Charlie was survived by three sons: Carson, Frederick, and Garret."

Boney rubbed his chin. "Maybe that's why he agreed to help us — we really did remind him of his sons."

Itchy furrowed his brow, chewing on the last of his

chocolate bar. "So . . . Charlie was a ghost pretending to be a man who was pretending to be a ghost . . ."

Squeak nodded.

"Once again, I'm totally confused."

Boney suddenly pointed to the door of the gymnasium. "Hey, Squeak, your dad's here!"

Squeak's father strode up, an adult version of Squeak, with his round face and big blue eyes. He smiled proudly, a big gap showing in his front teeth. "This is my boy," he said, throwing his arm around his son.

"Smile!" the journalist called out, his camera popping with a great big flash.

CHAPTER TWENTY-THREE

THE SWEET TASTE
OF SUCCESS

Boney lounged in the clubhouse, one foot dangling over the arm of his brand-new easy chair. Itchy sat at the table, stuffing his face with peanut butter and honey crackers, a can of pop in each hand. He selected a jar of chocolate sauce from the well-stocked clubhouse shelves and opened it, pouring sauce liberally overtop of his crackers. Squeak sat on the floor, organizing his stash of newly acquired special-effects gear. Henrietta scratched happily next to him, wearing a small, hand-knit sweater.

"This is the life," Itchy said, dribbling chocolate sauce onto his tongue. But he stopped mid-dribble as a familiar, hoarse laugh rose up from below. Itchy slammed down the jar of chocolate sauce and bolted to the window. It was Larry Harry with Jones and Jones, walking down the street.

"Hey, Larry," Itchy shouted down. "Look out for the ghost!"

Larry looked around in terror and began to run, with Jones and Jones stumbling frantically on his heels.

"Why don't you go steal some mail!" Itchy taunted.

Snuff burst out from behind some garbage cans and took up the chase, growling and snarling ferociously.

"Ahhhhh! Get it off me! Get it off meeeee!" Larry hollered as he ran.

Itchy shook his head. "Tsk, tsk . . . look at them go. You'd think they didn't like us or something."

Boney smiled. "I just might like that dog after all."

"Uh . . . guys," Squeak called from his place on the floor. "We've got a problem." He held Henrietta in the air. "She's a he."

Itchy scratched his head. "Huh?"

"She's a he," Squeak said again.

Itchy turned to Boney. "What's he talking about?"

"Henrietta is a Henry," Squeak explained. "I've been reading up on this, and our chicken isn't a hen at all, he's a rooster."

Boney raised his eyebrows. "Really?"

Squeak nodded. "Yep. No eggs for us."

Itchy scratched his arm thoughtfully. "Well . . . I guess it's a good thing we don't have to worry about

Prisoner 95 any more." He raised his cans of pop. "To Charlie," he said.

"To Charlie," Boney and Squeak toasted, raising their pop cans in the air.

Itchy guzzled from both cans, then wiped his mouth with a loud sigh. He looked at his friends happily.

"What should we do for the convention next year?" Boney asked.

"How about aliens?" Squeak said.

"As in UFOs?" Itchy gulped.

"Yeah, and other strange phenomena."

"That would be so cool!" Boney said.

Henry cheeped happily from the floor.

Itchy pulled on his wild red hair and groaned. "Oh, no, here we go again . . ."

THE END . . . ?

Thanks to my family and friends for their love and support. Thanks to my editor, Lynne Missen, and the entire staff at HarperCollins. Special thanks to Naomi and Doug, Akka, Chris and Richard, and my gal pal, Svetlana Chmakova.